BE
KEPT
SECRET

BEST KEPT SECRET

A Colorado Black Diamonds Novel

EMILY SILVER

To my dad and his hockey bros
Thanks for all your help with this book. But please don't ever help me
with titles again.
Like ever.

Welcome to the Colorado Black Diamonds!

While this series starts now, its roots are in the Denver Mountain Lions. The prologue was taken (and edited to fit this story) from Sideline Infraction to give you the backstory you need for Best Kept Secret!

Happy reading!
<3 Emily

Prologue

"Is it too much to ask you guys to shut the hell up? We've got a big game today and I'm trying to focus." I run a hand through my ragged hair.

"Oh shit. Something really did crawl up your ass." Colin's eyes drift to the other three crowding around my locker.

"What's got you so grumpy today?" Knox whips a towel in my direction.

"I'm fine."

"Everyone knows when someone says they're 'fine' they're not actually 'fine,'" Logan states matter-of-factly.

The tension in the locker room is high. Everyone is getting pumped for the game today. Especially since it's against Vegas. They're gunning for us today since we're leading the division.

But the tension sitting in my shoulders is for an entirely different reason. It's been a long few weeks.

Long, agonizing weeks without Carter.

I've never had anyone in my life like him before. Even

that brief shining glimpse of him was more than I could handle.

I've never felt so much love from one person before. Carter loved me for me. Not for the player I am. I was able to be myself with him. My true, nerdy, boy-band loving self.

And I threw that all away because I'm scared. Too scared to live my truth and be who I am. Because if anyone finds out I'm gay, how would the world react?

It's the same thought that keeps me up at night. Tossing and turning in my big empty bed.

Practice drained me of what little energy I have. It's like I'm moving through a swamp without him.

And every time I look at the coach, who just happens to be Carter's dad? It's like I'm looking at Carter in twenty years and everything I'll have missed out on in life. All because I'm letting the fear win.

"As long as his head is in the game, let him be," Jackson pipes up as he tugs his jersey on over his pads. "Alex knows what this game means."

Fuck.

As if anyone needed to add any more pressure to the weight on my shoulders.

I grab the eighteen jersey out of my locker, tracing the captain patch. In the last two weeks, I've felt like anything but a captain.

Snapping at anyone who dropped a pass or missed a block.

Fuck, Knox is right.

Except I'm way more than grumpy.

"Listen up, everyone." Coach's voice echoes around the locker room. The Mountain Lions logo on the floor beneath him looks like it's ready to swallow him whole.

"It's going to be a tough game out there today. Conditions are less than ideal. But we're used to the weather—it's nothing new. Plus we have home field advantage. So play your game and the rest will take care of itself."

I barely hear Knox's speech when he takes over from Coach before everyone empties out of the locker room. The noise of the crowd as we run out onto the field doesn't seem as loud as usual.

It's like everything is dull.

But not the icy rain. It's cutting as it soaks through the long-sleeved shirt underneath my pads.

Winter came early as my breaths are easy to see in the low light of the late afternoon. The stadium lights block out most of the crowd as we walk out to midfield for the coin toss.

Derek Hollins is out there for Vegas. His cocky grin as he shakes Colin's hand has me wanting to throw punches out here.

Bastard.

"Hopefully you're prepared to lose," he says, giving my hand an extra tight squeeze.

"Only losers here are you," Colin cuts in before I can.

"Gentlemen. We don't want to kick you out before the game." The ref eyes all of us. The game hasn't even started yet and they're out for blood. "Let's make it a good clean game."

Vegas wins the toss and defers to the second half.

"Your head in the game, Young?" Coach asks as I grab my helmet.

"Yes sir." I don't maintain eye contact, instead watching as our special teams returns the ball to the fifteen-yard line. Not great starting position in these conditions.

"Gutter Away Houston. Got it?" Williams, our offensive coordinator, pops up next to me.

I nod, running out onto the field.

"Good strong start, got it?" I eye each of my linemen and receivers.

"Let's shut them up!" Colin yells, pounding the pads of the closest player to him.

"Gutter Away Houston, on three. Break."

Everyone moves into position as I get behind my center. My eyes track the defense, not settling on any one player to give the play away.

Calling it, the center hikes the ball as I drop back, watching everything unfold before me. One of the line-backers gets around our tackle and I scramble. Backing up a few steps, I find Colin and throw the ball toward him.

The split-second delay allows him to only get six yards down the field before sliding out of bounds.

The weather isn't going to do us any favors as the next two plays don't gain us any yards.

Three and out. Worst possible way to start the game.

"Gonna be a long day for you, QB. A lot more where that came from," Hollins shouts as the lines switch up on the field. "Just you wait."

It takes everything I have to jog back to the sideline. All the tension inside of me is looking for a release. What I wouldn't give to be able to take it out on that dick.

But I can't do anything to jeopardize the game for my team.

For the first time in a long time, no one drops down next to me on the bench. It's like my aggression is radiating out from me and keeping everyone at bay.

But the nerves keep me from sitting still.

I pace on the sidelines as our defense tries to stop Vegas's offense from charging down the field. Instead, they steamroll right over us, easily taking the ball into the end zone.

Fuck. Vegas is off to a strong start, our fans voicing their distaste with boos.

"Alright boys. Time to get our heads in the game. Let's tie this up."

I get a few skeptical looks from the guys—because clearly it's my issue that's causing the team to flounder.

But it's only the first quarter. We can get those points back.

Rushing back onto the field, Vegas's D-line stops us on the first play.

Shit. Getting the guys back into the right headspace is going to be harder than I thought. Heads are hanging as they come back into the huddle.

"Alright. Let's shake it off. Charlie Blue Thirty on two." Everyone claps their hands, getting into position for the running play. It's going to be a fight to get every yard in this game with the rain coming down.

Snapping the ball, I complete an easy handoff to Logan, but not before Hollins comes at me. He pulls up a split second before plowing into me. The sneer on his face tells me he did it on purpose.

I should leave it. I should get back to the line and call a quick play to catch Vegas off guard. But I'm too on edge and have to poke the bear today.

"Play the damn ball, Hollins," I yell.

"Maybe if you were, you wouldn't be losing right now. Fucking fairy."

"What'd you say to me?" I'm in Hollins's face before I know what I'm doing. All I see is red.

"You heard me. Maybe if you weren't such a fairy you'd have an easier time staying on your feet."

"What the hell is your problem?" Kelly, our center, is right up next to me.

"Aww. Have to have your boyfriend defend you? Fucking queer," Hollins spits at me.

What tenuous grip I had on my sanity snaps and I'm punching Hollins to the ground.

Whistles and flags are being thrown as someone tries to pull me off him. Every ounce of pent-up sadness and anger is flying out of my fists. My helmet gets knocked off as Hollins swings a punch.

"You can do better than that," I egg him on. His knuckles crack my jaw.

"Fuck off, Young!"

"Aww, and here I thought you'd be a top." I give him my smarmiest smile.

"Get the fuck off me, you faggot!" This time, Hollins shoves me hard enough to knock me back off him, straight into the ref.

He's hauling me up while Hollins staggers to their side-lines. The crowd is booing all around me.

"...as a result, number eighteen of Denver and number twenty-two of Las Vegas have both been ejected from the game."

Kelly is shouting at the ref about what Hollins was saying, but I push him back to our side of the field. "We need you out there, man. Don't get kicked out too."

"You heard what he said to you, right? That can't slide!"

The anger that's clouding my brain starts to clear.

Fuck.

I just got kicked out of the game.

I've always been the levelheaded one on the field. I'm one of the captains of the team.

And with one jab from Hollins, I put everything I've worked my entire life for on the line.

Fuck.

By the time I make it back to the sideline, Coach is waiting for me, his face hard.

"You'll be waiting for me in my office when the game is over."

One of the team assistants escorts me back to the locker room. Whipping off my pads, they make a sickening crunch as they land in my locker, knocking everything out of place.

"Calm down, Young. Don't make this any worse." His words are harsh. I've earned them.

I can't remember ever feeling like this. I hit the showers, letting the water wash out every bitter thought I'm having.

Fucking fairy.

Fucking faggot.

Ejected from the game.

God, if Carter could see me now...except, he doesn't want to. And why would he want to see me like this?

This isn't who I am. I don't get tossed out of games. I don't fight words with fists.

I don't know who was on that field, but it definitely wasn't me.

Shutting the water off, I wrap a towel around my waist and head back to the locker room. I waste no time in getting dressed and then stomping off to the coach's office. I don't want to be in there when the team comes back in.

The looks on their faces will be too much to bear.

"IN ALL MY YEARS OF COACHING,"—COACH'S voice startles me from my slumped spot in a chair—"I have never seen anyone act like that on the field. Give me one good reason why I shouldn't bench you for the season."

Fuck. This is worse than I thought.

I give it to him straight. "He called me a faggot."

His face hardens. It's as if he's aged ten years right in front of me. "That's quite the accusation, Alex."

I shake my head. "Not an accusation, coach. Called me a fairy and a faggot. And I know I should be the bigger person, but I snapped. Hollins is a dick, Coach. We all know it."

"Dick or not, it doesn't mean you can go around unleashing your feelings on the players of this league."

"Right."

"Is there any reason that you would take these words to heart?"

Coach doesn't say anything else. He sits there with an assessing look in his eyes.

It sets my teeth on edge. It's like he can see straight through me.

Does he know I'm gay?

Does he know I broke his son's heart?

Sitting in front of this man, every reason I have for keeping my secret—my truth—to myself starts to whittle away.

What if I told him?

I study the man I've come to know in front of me. He's never guided me wrong. He never wavers in the face of insurmountable odds.

So tell him.

Wiping my hands on my pants, the tight ball of emotion bursts out of me.

"I'm gay."

"I see."

"And who I love shouldn't be an issue. But I'm not

naive enough to believe that there won't be more people like Hollins in the league who won't accept me for me. It doesn't matter because what happened today was that Hollins was a dick and his behavior shouldn't be tolerated."

"But your reaction to him wasn't appropriate either."

I stand, pacing the small room. It's only now that I hear the guys in the locker room. Instead of the boisterous tone of a win, it's somber. "We lost, didn't we?"

He nods his head. "Hard to come back when we lose our starting quarterback."

"Fuck!" I'm ready to punch the wall, but Coach comes around his desk, grabbing my shoulders and stopping me.

"Son, I'm going to give you a little advice."

I suck in a breath, waiting to hear his words.

"I'm going to tell you what I told my son when he came out to me. Life is hard, but who you choose to love shouldn't be. Choose your hard, Alex. Whether you choose to continue living in this closet you've built around yourself, or stepping out into the light, it's going to be hard either way. But wouldn't the hard be easier if you were happy?"

Every single emotion that I've been holding in for the last two weeks—hell, since I made the decision not to come out—comes flooding out. The dam bursts open, and I can't fight the tears as they come.

Coach pulls me in for a hug and I cling to him for dear life.

The number of people who know my sexuality? Four. My parents, Tommy, and Carter.

Now five.

Telling Coach was different. Carter knew. My parents and Tommy also knew. It wasn't hard coming out to them because they knew.

But Coach didn't. He's the first person I've made the conscious decision to tell.

A weight I always knew I was carrying lifts off me. I feel a hundred pounds lighter.

From telling one person.

Imagine what it will feel like if I come out to the world.

"You okay?" Coach pulls back.

I take a minute to wipe the tears and steady my breath. "I think so."

"Good. Anyone you can go home to?"

A furious blush creeps up my cheeks. "That ship has sailed."

The last thing I want to do is tell Coach that I've been sleeping with his son. Not that it matters anyway. We're not together.

"I'm sorry to hear that. Now, go home and don't talk to anyone until you hear from me. I'll talk with the team and try and get this sorted out."

I just hope it doesn't end with me getting my walking papers.

Chapter One

TROY

"I'm open! Pass the puck."

The tiny, black rubber disk slides across the gleaming ice. It lands with a crack in the cradle of my stick. Deking around the defenseman, I fly up the ice.

Pushing off my skates, my legs are screaming as I get closer to the net. It's only me and the goalie.

With practiced ease, I send the puck sailing through the air and watch as it thwacks against the back of the net.

"Hell yeah! That was a great start to practice, Gladiator!" My alternate captain, Marcus, calling me by my nickname, claps me on the shoulder. "If you play like that, we're going all the way!"

"Don't jinx us," someone calls out from next to us.

"Damn, that felt good, Wizard," I tell Marcus as I skate back to the bench to grab a swig from my water bottle.

I'm breathing hard. No amount of training can ever prepare you for those first weeks of hockey practice after the offseason.

Endless sprints. Skating back and forth across the rink. My legs and lungs are on fire.

We're only just getting started.

It's my senior year. My last chance to try and win a championship with the San Diego University Sand Sharks. We made it to the Frozen Four last year, but failed to advance to the finals.

It fucking sucked. If I have anything to say about it this year, we're making it all the way.

The last banner hanging in the rafters was from before my time here. SDU is one of the top division one hockey schools in the country. Names of Hall of Fame players line the walls in the rink. Pictures from championship eras in the past stare us down as we practice. The arena is rife with history from how good our school is.

It stings more than it should that I haven't added a banner up there.

"Let's change up the lines," our coach calls out. I skate over the Sand Shark in the center of the ice and hit the bench.

He's a man of few words. Someone you desperately want to impress, but never want that stern eye looking at you for too long.

Coach Morris has been with the Sand Sharks longer than I've been alive. Or at least it seems that way. With his fast graying hair, he's looking that much closer to retirement.

But I know he wants to win a championship as much as I do.

The freshmen take the ice and I study them.

"Do you think we ever looked that green?" Marcus asks from beside me.

"Fuck no. They get younger every year."

"Careful, boys,"—the assistant coach slaps us on the shoulder—"you're starting to sound old."

"Not that old," Marcus mumbles next to me.

I go back to studying the new talent. Even if we haven't won a championship in the last three years, we're one of the top teams in the country. Top hockey players from all over want to come here and play for us. Everyone here is lucky to have made the cut.

"Change it up!" Coach shouts from behind us, and Marcus and I leap over the boards to get back on the ice.

We ease into our positions and take off down the ice. Between the two of us, we know where the other is going to be on instinct. We've played together long enough to know.

A winger comes in and grabs the puck before it can make it to Marcus. Sneaky bastard.

I take off after them to try and steal it back, but he's a blur of red and black on the ice. He gets an easy goal on the backup goalie.

"Hell yeah!" Isaac cheers. He's a sophomore who is hoping to move up to second line this year.

"Don't get cocky, Isaac," Marcus tells him.

"Getting one on you two?" He flips a gloved finger back and forth between the two of us. "I'm going to savor this."

"Yeah, yeah." I skate back to center ice to get ready to start the drill when Coach calls everyone to the bench.

"Alright, men." Coach looks at each and every one of us. "I know it's been a long first month back. It's early, but I like how we're looking. We have our first game next week, and I don't know about you, but I'm ready to get back out there and show everyone what we Sand Sharks can do. We got close last year, but this year? I want us to go all the way."

"Hell yeah!" someone shouts from behind me.

"I want you to stick together as a team. Work hard,

study harder, and we'll do great things this season. Now hit the showers."

"Great work, boys." I hit the pads of a few guys as they head toward the locker room.

"Troy. A word?" Coach asks.

"What's up?" I lean against my stick as he waits for the rink to empty around us.

"I got an email from one of your professors."

"Okay." I gulp down a cold breath of air. That's never a good way to start a conversation. "Which one?"

"Astronomy. They're worried you're falling behind."

"I promise, I'm trying, Coach."

"It's only a few weeks into the semester. Don't dig yourself a hole you can't get out of. You know my policy."

"I know. I'll make sure I don't."

"Good. Now get out of here."

Fuck. I head down the tunnel to the locker room, my mood souring fast. School has never come easy to me. And if my grades start dropping, I'll lose my starting position. It's Coach's way of making sure we don't slack off in our academics. It's never been an issue before, but with only two semesters between me and graduating, a lot could happen. Like scouts not seeing me play.

The mood in the locker room is boisterous as music blares from a portable speaker. Red carpeting lines the circular locker room floor. The Sand Sharks mascot sits in the center of the floor—something no one ever steps on unless you want the team to lose.

Wooden lockers line the walls with lights to show off everyone's name. It's the nicest locker room I've ever been in.

Grabbing my towel from my locker, I strip out of my gear and head toward the showers. The last thing I wanted was to start this year off on the wrong foot. It seems no matter what I do, it's not good enough.

Hockey comes easy to me. It's everything else that I struggle with. I put off the classes I didn't want to take until now, figuring it might be easier. Of course I got the hardest professors who don't take shit from anyone.

And now it might royally fuck me over.

Taking a quick shower, I wrap the towel around my waist and head back into the locker room.

"You up for going out tonight, Troy?"

"Can't. I have my calc test to study for tomorrow and an astronomy paper to write."

"Already? It's only the third week of school." Marcus eyes me like he can't believe it.

"Shit. You have Professor Smith, don't you? He's a dick," Isaac chirps from down the bench.

I nod my head. "He really is."

"Dude, Gladiator, he has it out for hockey players."

"Not just hockey players, all athletes," Marcus quips. "He hates any student athlete."

"Great," I moan.

It's going to be a long semester if these first few weeks are anything to go by. Math has always been my worst subject in school. No matter how many tutors I've gotten, it never makes sense. I can do just enough to skate by, but I don't know with this professor.

And if I want to stay on the team and not risk my chances of going pro, I'm going to need to buckle down and study every chance I get.

"You sure you don't want to go out? I'm sure there'll be some chicks to pick up." Randy waggles his eyebrows at me. Dude has never met a puck bunny he turns down. He gets around more than any guy on the team.

"Can you show them a little more respect?" I roll my eyes at him. Jesus, sometimes these guys can be assholes.

"You're really telling me you'll pass up a chance for some ass tonight to study?"

He says it like it's the worst thing in the world.

"Yes. Because if I fail calc, then I can't play." I pull my T-shirt on over my head. "I'll see you guys later."

Grabbing my backpack, I head out of the locker room and into the bright, San Diego afternoon.

Campus is tucked away near the beach, like its own little city within a city. It's one of the reasons I love it here so much. Best hockey program in the nation notwithstanding, it's quiet. It doesn't feel like you're in the middle of a big city.

Cutting my way through campus, I head to the library. Everyone is out in the quad soaking in the sun. Palm trees line the sidewalks between Spanish-style buildings. The library is one of the newer buildings on campus, and probably the ugliest. It's one big square made from cinderblock.

Heading inside, I'm met with a wall of cold air.

"Hey Troy!" A blonde wiggles her fingers at me as I enter the library.

"Hi."

"Going to be a good season?"

"I hope so."

I don't let the conversation linger. Being the team captain, I get more people I don't know approaching me than I know what to do with.

Especially the ladies. It's not me being cocky—it's the truth. I get so many women throwing themselves at me that it wears me out.

With it being my senior year, and the most important year with scouts coming to see me play, I don't want to be distracted.

But as I set my backpack down on a small table in the corner of the second floor, a certain brunette catches my eye.

One that I don't know, yet I know everything about.

Angela Brooks-Young.

She's the same age as I am. A senior. Somehow, on this campus, our paths have hardly ever crossed. I never see her at the hockey games or parties. I have no idea where she spends her free time.

It's like my thoughts of her pull her attention to mine. Caramel-brown eyes flit up to look at me.

I don't miss the subtle way her gaze narrows on mine. More of a glare, really.

There is no love lost between our families. Her dad hates mine. Growing up, I knew all about her family. It's hard not to when the teams your dads played for were bitter rivals.

Long, brown hair falls around her face. It doesn't hide the way her eyes keep seeking mine.

Angela Brooks-Young. The one person I wouldn't mind getting to know better. Except I can't. That's not where my focus needs to be.

Hockey. That's my biggest priority this year. My *only* priority.

Like I said, I don't need the distraction.

Chapter Two

ANGIE

"Is that right? I feel like it's wrong."

"That's exactly it!" I cheer on the high school student I'm working with.

"It is? I can't believe I did that."

"Proofs get easier as you do them."

She shakes her head. "I don't know why we have to prove a problem is right. Seems dumb."

I laugh. "You're telling me. I hated proofs, but now that I understand them, they aren't so bad."

"Well, maybe I'll get at least a B on my test this week."

"You will."

The phone on the table between us buzzes. "Mom's here. Thanks, Angie!"

"Bye, Megan!"

I smile after her retreating form. She's bright. One of the few high school students I tutor while working here at the academic center.

It's something I've loved doing since I got to SDU. I love being able to help people. The tutoring center, with all of its books and academic posters lining every inch of

"And it's Friday. You're fine!" Her voice is indignant. "Weren't you telling me you wanted to have more fun this year?"

I twist my face at her. "More fun? I don't think I said that to you."

"I think you did." Harper taps a perfectly manicured pink nail on her lips. "You practically begged me to drag you out to more parties this year."

I close my laptop and look over at her. "Now I know you're lying."

"Fine. But will you please come with me somewhere? I need a wing woman," she begs.

Based on the pleading look on her face, I know I'm not going to like where she wants to take me. But it's hard to deny your best friend something that she clearly wants.

"Where are we going and do I have time to change beforehand?"

I look down at the simple black T-shirt I'm wearing with cut-off jean shorts. My brown hair is haphazardly thrown up into a long ponytail. Since I don't have class on Fridays, I opted for no makeup.

Not exactly ready to be going out wherever she plans on taking me.

"Please. You look gorgeous as is." Harper helps me by shutting my books and stowing them in my backpack. "There's the pep rally tonight for the hockey team that I want to hit up."

"Ugh, really?"

I hate hockey. Possibly more than any sport on the planet.

Harper holds her hands up in defense. It's then I notice she looks much nicer than she usually does for an afternoon filled with classes.

Today, she's dressed in tight jeans, an SDU hockey shirt, and has her hair and makeup done.

"Look, I know you hate hockey players, but please? There's someone I really want to see on the team."

"Who?" I ask. Gathering up the last of my things, we leave the tutoring center behind us.

"Marcus Evans."

"Of course you'd go for the captain."

"Alternate, Ang. He's the alternate. You know I like men in power positions."

I snort laugh as the sun hits us both in the face. Fishing my sunglasses out of my bag, I let her lead me in the direction we have to go.

"Is it really a power position if he's the alternate?"

"Oh, honey. You wouldn't like who's the captain."

"I know I don't."

Because I know exactly who the captain of the hockey team is.

Troy Hollins.

The son of the man who made my dad's life miserable when he was in the NFL. I heard all about Derek Hollins growing up.

His son, Troy?

Bad news. Stay away. Far, far away.

"Tsk. I'd expect better from you, Angela Brooks-Young."

"I don't have to like everyone."

But I usually do. Ever since I was little, I've never met a stranger. I guess it was in my nature, growing up in the public spotlight as I did with a dad who was a Super Bowl winning quarterback for the Denver Mountain Lions.

"You are so stubborn."

The closer we get to the ice rink, the more my nerves are starting to ratchet up. Crowds are gathering outside where a stage is set up. Speakers sit on either side so whoever is at the podium can be heard.

"I'm not stubborn because I don't like hockey players, Harper."

"I believe the term you've used is 'the scourge of the earth.'"

That gets a laugh out of me. "Hey, I'm here with you, aren't I?"

Just because I have issues with hockey players doesn't mean I can't support my friend. Even if they have burned me in the past.

One specific hockey player. One I wish I'd never met.

We find a spot in the crowd right as the team comes onto the stage.

"There he is!" Harper points to one of two guys that are standing in front of everyone else.

The man in question is tall with a broad chest. Tattoos peek out on each bicep from under his hockey tee. He has thick, wavy brown hair and scruff that lines his jaw.

"Isn't he gorgeous?"

I don't hear her question, nodding because the man my eyes are now focused on has stepped up to the microphone.

"What's up, Sand Sharks?!" Troy calls out to the eagerly waiting fans. People are cheering loudly as he waves his arms to get them even louder.

I'm not one of them. I stand there, arms crossed, watching as everyone loses their minds for the hockey team. People love hockey here.

Especially a small group of women standing near us. I do my best to ignore them talking about how much they want to sleep with all of the players.

I hate that he's so captivating. Every single person here is listening to what he's saying. I've missed most of it, so lost in thought studying him.

Sure, Marcus is good-looking, but Troy is on a whole other level. If he wasn't a hockey player, he'd be exactly my type.

Tall, but not too tall. Brown hair that falls into his eyes. Strong arms and thick thighs that are no doubt thanks to his hockey training.

It's annoying how good-looking I find him. I shouldn't even be noticing this man.

"We've got our first game of the season tomorrow, and we can't wait to see you all in the stands!"

More cheers.

More eye rolls from me.

"Make sure you wear your best Sand Shark gear to help cheer us on to a victory!"

Harper erupts next to me before the coach says a few words, then the marching band starts to play. The team disperses, making their way through the crowd.

"C'mon. I want to say hi to Marcus." Harper grabs me by the arm and drags me through the thick throng of people.

"I'll wait here."

"Oh, you big baby."

Because I see exactly who is trailing behind Marcus. I have no desire to run into him today. Or ever, really.

Troy Hollins is off-limits. A no go. Danger zone.

And that's exactly how I intend him to stay.

Chapter Three

TROY

"**Y**ou ready for class today, Gladiator?"

I drop down into the seat next to Marcus in our astronomy class.

"I spent all night studying for my calc test this afternoon, so no. Maybe you need to give me some of that magic you're known for."

Marcus is one of our best players when it comes to closing out close games. It's why we deemed him The Wizard.

"Better hope there isn't a pop quiz today." Marcus elbows me in the side.

"Dude, really? Don't even joke about that."

I pull out my notes as class fills up around us. The science building is old, with hardwood floors and even harder chairs in the auditorium our class is in. Seats creak as the room fills up as we get closer to the start of class.

It has that old college smell.

Like paper and fear.

We're only a few weeks into the semester but I already

feel behind. Hockey has taken up most of my focus, so I haven't given school the attention I should be.

Getting an athletic scholarship means I have to keep my grades up. I took astronomy because everyone on the team said it was an easy A.

Easy A, my ass.

I've never had to work so hard in my life at anything. Plus with Coach Morris being on me now, it's going to get even worse.

If only studying came as easily as hockey.

It's the only thing I'm good at. The only possible future I've ever thought about.

A future that might not come to pass because of astronomy and Professor Craig.

I groan, throwing my head back and trying to shake off the feeling of incompetence. Marcus is talking to someone on his other side when my eyes land on the door.

And the brunette that's walking into class.

Angie.

Fuck.

I hate that my eyes automatically follow her through the hall as she takes a seat in the front of the class. She's flanked by two other girls.

No doubt they're all brainiacs. Because who else would sit in the front row by choice?

"Forget about it, Hollins." Marcus pulls my attention away from the one woman I can't help but sit up and take notice of.

I don't want to. I don't *want* to want her.

But I do.

There's something about her that intrigues me. Maybe it's because she's off-limits.

"I don't know what you're talking about." I lean down,

grabbing a piece of gum from my backpack and popping it in my mouth.

"You can't have her."'"

"Who? I seriously don't know what you're talking about."

Marcus laughs, a skeptical noise. He's my closest friend on the team. At SDU really. We got here at the same time as freshmen and clicked on the first day. He doesn't put up with the shit from the other guys. Sure, we like to go to parties together, but it's not all we live for.

He's like me, here on a scholarship. Except school comes much easier to Marcus than it does to me.

"Bro, you couldn't be more obvious if you tried."

I flit my gaze to him. "I'm not being obvious about anything."

He laughs in my face.

Asshole.

"If that's what you want to believe."

I go back to ignoring him.

He acts like I've been obsessing over Angie. Which is the furthest thing from the truth. In all the time we've been on campus together, this is the first time we've ever had a class together. I've seen her every now and then.

And every time, I can't help but drink my fill of her.

Maybe I'm a masochist.

I can't have her. But every time, she leaves me wanting more.

"Pop quiz. Books away." Professor Craig walks into the room, his gray eyebrows drawn tight under his glasses. "You'll have twenty minutes before we start today's lesson."

His clipped tone makes me dislike our professor even more than I already do.

Fuck me.

available space, is like a second home to me. It's where I spend most of my time outside of my own classes.

Taking the geometry books back to their shelves, I grab a few more for my own classes to start getting ahead.

Even though it's my senior year, professors aren't letting us slack off. We're only a few weeks into the semester, and I have two papers and an exam coming up in the next two weeks. If I don't take it seriously, I won't be graduating with honors.

Not that anyone would be disappointed if I didn't. My grades are good enough that my dads wouldn't care what happened. They'll be proud of me either way. My godfather, Colin, on the other hand? I was told to break the rules this year, otherwise *he* would be disappointed in me.

I laugh, grabbing my laptop to start on my astronomy paper. It's one of my favorite classes so far. I needed it to finish my science requirements, and since it's freshman level, it's easy enough for me to grasp the material.

"I thought I'd find you in here." Peering up from my book, I smile as my roommate drops into the seat across from me.

"Hey Harper."

She is the epitome of a SoCal bombshell. Tan skin, long, blonde hair, and bright blue eyes that are always sparkling. With a permanent smile on her face, nothing can ever get her down.

"I thought you were going to cut back on your hours in here?" She grabs my book and flips through it.

"*You* told me I needed to cut back on my hours. It doesn't count if I'm working on my own homework."

Harper rolls those big blue eyes at me. "It's our senior year, Ang. You need to have fun."

"It doesn't mean I can't finish my paper. It needs to be done by Monday."

"You just had to say it, didn't you?" I shake my head at Marcus.

The last thing I need is a pop quiz when I spent all night studying for calc.

"You know me saying it didn't make it happen, right?"

"Might as well have."

I grab the remote we use for pop quizzes in class and start reading through the questions that are projected on the screen. I hate these because I know immediately if I pass or fail. The last time we had one, I did not do well.

This class is kicking my ass, and the further along in the semester we get, the harder it's going to be to get my grade up.

Half of the questions on the screen seem like they're in a foreign language.

Calculate the number of light years away a star is?

How does a black hole form?

What is the difference between a nebula and a galaxy?

With each passing question, my mind spins. I have no idea if I'm answering any of these questions correctly.

"Remotes away." Professor Craig changes the screen to start reviewing the information. "Please get out your computers so we can review the information."

I log into our campus-wide system and pull up this class.

D.

Fuck me. And what's even worse is there's an empty grade where my most recent paper should be.

"Has he graded this yet?" I lean over to Marcus and ask him.

"Yeah, why?"

"Great."

My mood takes a further nosedive as Professor Craig

breezes through the material like everyone in the room should have any clue what he's talking about.

I'm sure most are following along, but trying to take notes and keep up with him? I feel like I'm in my own black hole right now.

There's nothing more demoralizing than sitting through a class where you feel like you're losing brain cells. I can't follow a single thing the professor is talking about. I'm sure he gets some kind of joy out of making students feel like this.

Had I known this class would be this hard, I would've found something else to take. Not suffer through feeling like a bigger idiot every time I'm in class.

"Next class, we'll be reviewing for the first exam of the semester. I suggest you all come prepared, as we will be working in small groups to review the information." His eyes land on me, and I take it as a direct hit.

What a dick. I hate professors like him. He clearly gets off on making students miserable.

Books and laptops are slammed shut as the sound of desks getting folded back into their seats reverberates around the room. The chatter of the departing students fills the air around me when I hear the voice I loathe.

"Mr. Hollins. A word?" Professor Craig asks.

Class empties out around me as I remain in my seat. No sense in hurrying out if I have to stay here. I take my time stowing everything in my backpack, trying to ease the nerves now raging in my stomach.

"See you at home?" Marcus asks, hiking his backpack farther up his shoulder.

I blow out a frustrated breath. "Yeah. See ya later."

By the time the last student leaves, I make my way down to the front of the auditorium where Professor Craig is leaning against the desk.

He can't be that much older than my dad. Early fifties, maybe? He has the hardened look of a professor who has taken too much shit from too many students and doesn't want to hear another excuse from anyone.

"Mr. Hollins. Do you know why I asked to see you today?"

"I'm not sure." I hold on to the straps of my backpack, needing something to do with my hands so I don't fidget.

"Your most recent paper"—he pulls it out of a file on his desk—"was unable to be graded."

"Unable to grade? What do you mean? I worked hard on this." I snatch the paper from his outstretched hand. It's ten pages filled with red marks and lines.

"As such," he ignores me, continuing on, "it does not show a grasp of any of the material we have reviewed so far in the course of the semester."

"So why didn't you just give me an F then if it was so terrible?" It's hard to keep my voice even.

Does he have to be such a pompous jackass?

"You need to pass, yes?"

"I do." No sense in lying to him.

"Otherwise you'll lose your starting position on the soccer puck team."

"Hockey."

He waves me off. "It's all the same to me. Because I am a forgiving person, I am going to give you another chance."

Forgiving, my ass.

"I need to rewrite this?"

Professor Craig nods. "Get help, a study partner, anything and give me something I can grade. I expect this by Monday."

"Four days? We had two weeks the last time."

"Then you better get started." He snaps his briefcase closed and walks out the door.

"Jackass," I mutter at the closed door.

God. If only I didn't make a promise to my parents to finish college and get a degree. With my dad only playing for a few years in the NFL, he wanted me to have the best shot of a future after my playing career ended. I could be playing for the pros now instead of figuring out how the hell I'm going to pass a class that everyone told me I could sleep my way through.

Dejection hangs heavy on my shoulders as I leave the science building. Between astronomy and calculus, I'll be lucky to keep my starting position on the hockey team.

Forget that. Not just my starting position, but my position at all.

The sun is irritatingly bright this afternoon. Groups of students are clustered around the quad. A few wave to me as I take the familiar route back to the hockey house.

Except…studying there isn't going to get me anywhere. I clearly don't know the material like I thought I did.

Instead of going home to sulk before practice, I head to the student center. There's no way I'm going to give up my starting position on the hockey team without a fight.

The all-glass building sits in the middle of campus. It's a bit of an eyesore with the way the sun reflects off it. With the sun beating down, I'm hit with a wall of heat as I walk inside.

Finding the map of the building, I locate the tutoring center and head that way. Never, in all my years of being here, have I needed help. I've mostly been able to coast through the last three years. Clearly Professor Craig isn't going to give me any leeway. Most professors give a lot of grace to student athletes. Not that I ever expected it, but it helped to have an extra day or two on papers while traveling for away games.

By the time I make it where I need to be, my nerves are getting the best of me. I hate this feeling. Like I'm a failure. It feels like every pair of eyes tracked me here. That there's a giant, neon sign hanging above my head that I'm failing two of my classes.

Pushing open the door, I'm met with a face I recognize. One that instantly drops into a frown.

"What are you doing here?" Angie asks, dropping the pen in her hand.

Not the most welcoming person. I let out a sigh. It was already hard enough to come here, so this doesn't bode well for me.

"Uhh." I scrub my hand down the back of my neck. "I need help."

"With what?" she bites back. Ouch. I'm not used to someone outright hating me like this.

"Astronomy. Calc. You name it, I need help."

Her eyes study me. I don't know her, but it's clear she's putting a wall between us. This is the first time I've ever spoken to her, and I can tell she hates me.

"You're not here to make fun of anyone?" Her brown hair is pulled back in a sleek ponytail. The red SDU T-shirt she wears shows off the freckles on her arms.

"Why would I do that?"

She crosses her arms. "Because people have come in here before to make fun of students who need help."

"Well, that's a dick move." I reach back into my bag to pull out my astronomy paper, debating if I should show her. She could use this against me. Tell everyone what an idiot I am.

Not that hockey players have a reputation for being the smartest people on the planet.

Swallowing what little pride I have left, I hand the paper over to her.

"I have to turn something in by next week or I'll fail this."

Angie's nose twists up as she flips through the paper. "You said you also needed help with calculus? Who's your professor?"

"Smith."

Angie nods, setting the paper down on the counter that separates the two of us.

"I have someone that can help you there, but no one for Craig's class."

"Aren't you in my same class?"

"I can't help you."

I guess this is going to be harder than I thought.

"Please. You have to help me. If I fail this class, I'll get kicked off the hockey team."

Apparently I'm not above begging.

"You will?"

I shrug a shoulder. "Yeah. Coach says if we can't maintain Cs, then we won't be able to maintain our starting positions."

"So not kicked off the team, then," Angie oh-so-helpfully points out. "You just won't be a starter."

"Same difference."

She thrusts my paper back at me, pushing it against my chest. Angie pulls back, like she's been burned. "Look, I can't help you."

"Can't or won't?"

"Does it matter?"

"Apparently not," I grumble. "Why bother helping at the tutoring center if you're not going to help people?"

"That's not fair." I hate how indignant her tone sounds. Like I'm the one causing problems.

"So you're going to help me then?"

Angie shakes her head, clearly not comfortable with this conversation either. "Look, I can have someone help you with Professor Smith's class, but I'll ask around to find someone for astronomy."

I stare at her, trying to figure out if she'll change her mind. But it doesn't seem like she will. I don't know why I came here.

"Don't bother. I'll figure something out."

"Troy, wait."

I don't turn back, hand held steady on the door. "This was a mistake. I don't want your help."

And with that, I leave.

Not quite sure what the fuck I'm supposed to do now.

Chapter Four

ANGIE

W hy can't this year be easy? It's my senior year. I want it to be simple. No drama, nothing.

And then Troy has to come walking into the tutoring center today and throw me off my game. He turned me into a blubbering idiot.

I don't know how I put more than two sentences together. All I know is I told him I couldn't help and that was it.

Except the look on his face is one I can't forget.

Dejected. Hurt. Embarrassed.

Stop stewing, Angie. It's not going to help anyone.

Parking my car, I grab my purse and head into the bar to meet Harper.

It's one of the newer bars on campus. Brick walls are filled with planters that overflow with greenery. Old chandeliers hang throughout the small bar. Mismatched tables and chairs fill the space. A patio lines one wall that opens up to the warm night.

Spotting Harper, she's at our usual hightop table beyond the bar.

"Hey. Sorry I'm late. My lecture ran late after tutoring this afternoon."

"It's fine." Harper waves me off as I slide onto a stool beside her. "I ordered you a beer."

"Thanks." I grab the icy glass in front of me and drink a healthy swallow. "It was a long day."

"Tutoring not going well?"

I shake my head, setting the glass down. "You'll never guess who came in today."

"Who?" Harper pops one of the pretzels on the table in front of us.

"Troy Hollins."

"Seriously?" Her jaw drops. "Why'd he come in?"

"Why do you think? He needs help in a couple of classes." I grab my own pretzel and munch on it.

"Who's going to help him?"

"Not me," I scoff. "I don't know who is going to help him."

"Angie." Harper's tone tells me I'm not going to like what she's about to tell me. "Why aren't you helping him?"

"Why do you assume it has to be me?"

"Why else would you be bringing it up?"

I take another sip of my beer in lieu of answering. I don't tell a lot of people no. Only the ones who have classes that I don't understand. But I couldn't in good conscience tell him yes.

"I don't think I've ever seen you tell someone no before."

"It's not like I have to say yes to everyone. I wouldn't have enough time for my own classes. Besides, I was cutting back on tutoring anyway."

"Were you?" Harper raises a skeptical brow in my direction. "How many times have you told yourself that today?"

"Get out of my head, Harper."

She shrugs, taking an easy sip of her own drink. "I'm just saying, it's not like you to turn down someone who needs help."

"I can't."

The words taste sour in my mouth. I told him no.

So why does it feel so bad?

"If that's what you need to tell yourself to feel better about it."

"Harper."

"What? I'll stop saying anything."

"Because you've already said so little." I finish my beer and flag down the passing server to order another. If this is how the night is going to continue, I'm going to need more to drink.

"I'll stop talking now."

"You will?"

Harper mimes zipping her lips and only smiles at me. It won't last long. She's the chattiest person I've ever met.

My second beer gets dropped off and she pipes up. "Thank you."

"I think that's a new record for you." I laugh.

"Thirty seconds? I can do better than that."

"Does that mean you're going to ignore me all night?"

"Not going to ignore you. Even if I disagree with your decision."

"Why don't you tell me about your day?" I try to change the subject.

"I hung out with Marcus."

Great. Another topic I really don't enjoy discussing.

Hockey players.

"Are you and Marcus a thing now?"

"I hope we're a thing. He's great, Angie. I know you don't like players, but he's not one."

"If you say so."

"Maybe the three of us can hang out."

"As long as it's only the three of us."

"I have no ulterior reasons for wanting to hang out."

"Not even considering who his best friend is?"

If this is her way of trying to get Troy in good with me, I'm not falling for it. Marcus and Troy are captains on the hockey team. Even if I don't follow it, I know that much as often as it's mentioned around campus.

You'd think the two of them were gods with how much people worship them. Something I've never given in to.

"Just want my best friend to get to know the guy I like."

"I can do that."

"Good. Want him to meet us now?"

"Oh my God, Harper! Is he just hanging out at the bar right now?" I look around, expecting him to pop out at our side. Like a magician pulling a rabbit out of a hat.

"What? No. I was going to text him to meet us." She holds up her phone.

"Just him." I point at her, taking a sip of my beer.

It's all I'll have tonight, so I need to pace myself. I shouldn't be so nervous meeting Harper's new boyfriend, or the guy she likes. I don't know what she's calling him.

I just don't want the conversation to turn back to Troy. Even just the thought of him has me hot under the collar.

"Are you nervous to meet him?" Harper asks, pulling me from my thoughts.

"No. Why?"

She spins a finger in my face. "Because you're blushing."

"Am not."

I totally am. I can feel it. All because of thoughts of some guy who shouldn't be making me feel like this.

This really is going to be the worst year if this keeps happening.

So much for easy.

Chapter Five

ANGIE

I flip back to the business textbook open on my desk next to my laptop. My eyes are dry and scratchy from staring at my computer all day.

Senior year has been anything but easy. With a double major in business and social work, my workload is heavy. My business class is taking up most of my time. The project for the semester is to start a business from scratch and plan everything that goes into getting it off the ground.

And with a paper due on Monday, I've been working most of the afternoon away.

A familiar name lights up my phone, pulling a smile from me as I shut my laptop with one final section left.

"Hey Dad."

"Here I thought you'd forgotten about me and Pops."

I roll my eyes at him, even though he can't see me. "Maybe if you didn't call me during class I could talk to you."

"I guess I can't complain that you take your education seriously."

"A trait I get from Pops."

"That you do," he laughs. "How are your classes going?"

"Top of the class in everything."

"That's my girl. Just make sure tutoring doesn't get in the way of your own studies."

I gulp down the guilt at remembering Troy's face when I told him I couldn't help him. That's not who I am. My dad—well, both of my dads—raised me to always help others.

But what would they say if I was helping Derek Hollins's son?

I don't even want to think about that.

"I won't." I shift the phone to my other ear. "Harper and I went to the football game today."

Dad groans over the phone. "SDU is not looking good this year."

"If only they had a quarterback of your level."

A crackle comes from the other end of the line. "Angie, don't give your dad a big head," comes Pops's voice.

"Hey Pops. Don't worry, it can't get any bigger."

"Hey!" Dad chirps over the phone. "I'm right here."

"It's a good thing there's other good teams here I can support."

"Just not hockey," Pops says.

"Don't worry, I won't become a hockey fan anytime soon."

Too much history there to even fathom going to a game. No matter how good San Diego University's hockey team is.

"Any big plans this weekend?"

"Harper and I are going to a party tonight."

"Make sure you have your phone with you," they tell me in unison.

I laugh at them. Over two decades of being married and they really have become the same person. No matter where I am, they are always worrying about me, something I don't think is going to change despite my age.

"I will. And we don't leave without letting each other know."

"There are some things I wish we didn't have to know," Dad says.

"You asked. I'm not going to lie to you."

"It's why you're the best daughter in the world, Angela." I can hear the smile in Pops's voice.

Harper comes into my room and flops down on my queen bed. "I have to go. Harper is giving me the evil eye."

Even though she's not, I know this conversation could go on all night.

"We love you, sweetheart. Talk soon."

"Love you, bye."

I end the call and move to sit beside her. It's nice we each have our own room and bathroom. We don't have to cram together. The apartment is an open floor plan, with each of us having our own space on separate ends of the kitchen and living room.

"Talking with your dads?"

I nod. "They're just checking in with me. I haven't talked to them in a few days."

Harper scoffs. "Heaven forbid you don't check in daily."

"Hey!" I poke her with my sock-clad foot. "Just because I like talking with them doesn't mean I have to check in daily."

"I think I talk with my parents maybe once a month?"

It's something Harper has always thought was weird. From the first day we met freshman year, I've talked to my dads every few days. Our family is close. We always have been. It's not something I've ever apologized for.

I know how lucky I am to have them. Both of them. Even my annoying little brother.

"What time are we leaving tonight?" I ask, changing the subject, messing with the gray-and-pink duvet on my bed.

"Want to head to the food court and grab something to eat before we head out?"

I nod. "Sounds good to me."

"Perfect!" Harper jumps up, slapping me on the side of my leg. "Get ready. And wear something hot!"

"I can't believe I let you talk me into this."

Harper links her arm through mine as we walk through campus. It's a warm night.

"You need to get out of your comfort zone. Besides, you look hot and should show that off."

"I let you take me to parties all the time." I look down at my dark, ripped skinny jeans, black top with puff sleeves that shows a sliver of my stomach, and black pointy heels. I love this outfit. It makes me feel sexy without showing off too much.

"Because otherwise you'd be holed up in your room studying all the time!"

I roll my eyes at her as we turn down the road where the hockey house is. "I do more than study, Harper. I just don't like hockey parties. And I've already had my max of hockey players to last me a lifetime."

"Marcus invited me. I knew you'd say no if you knew."

"If you told me that, I would've said yes."

"How magnanimous of you."

I laugh, squeezing her closer to me. "I'm a good friend like that."

Harper gives me a peck on the cheek as the house comes into view. "The very best."

Loud music is blasting out of a few houses. This street is filled with nothing but athletic housing. The baseball team takes up one end of the street, followed by football, soccer, then hockey.

"Who knows? Maybe we'll both get lucky tonight." Harper winks at me.

"I doubt it."

I've become jaded over the years. Something that's hard at the ripe old age of twenty-two. Everyone always had an agenda. And with who my dad is, I got a lot of fuck boys wanting to date me. They thought because I'm the daughter of Denver's Hall of Fame quarterback Alex Young that I'd get them an introduction. One too many times made me decide to stay single.

It would take a lot for me to start dating someone, and Harper is well aware of this.

"Time to get our party on!" Harper shouts.

People are crowded on the front porch of the house, red Solo cups in hand as we head inside. With the hockey team being SDU's most popular team, their parties are always the place to be.

If, you know, that's your thing.

Which it's not mine.

I don't like hockey players and it's about as good as walking into the lion's den for me.

A wall of sound slams into us as we walk inside, causing me to wince. The house is packed with wall-to-wall people. Beat-up pieces of furniture line one wall with old hockey posters hanging above them. SDU Sand Shark banners hang between Christmas lights from the ceiling. It looks like every college house you can imagine.

"I'll grab us some drinks," Harper yells in my ear over the music.

I nod and squeeze through the crush of people. Bodies are sticky with sweat, grinding against one another. I recognize a few people, waving at them as I try to find a quiet spot in all the madness.

Before I know what's happening, someone grabs my wrist and pulls me into them.

"Hey there, sexy. Looking for me?" The smarmy voice sends goose bumps over my skin.

"Not a chance in hell."

"You sure? I know you've been dreaming about me." I spin in this person's arms, his hands dropping low on my ass.

Brown eyes are glazed over, and his breath reeks of tequila.

This right here is why I hate college parties. It's fun going out with Harper and our friends, but guys like this one make it unbearable.

"I haven't thought about you at all, actually." I shove his hands off me.

"Oh, come on now. Don't be like that."

"I'll be however I want. I didn't ask for you to come on to me."

"God, what a bitch."

"Excuse me?" That gets a rise out of me.

I can handle a drunk college boy. My dads made me take self-defense before college for safety reasons. I've never had to use those skills before.

Right now? Right now, I'm veering dangerously close to kicking this guy in the balls.

He wraps a hand around my waist and pulls me back in to him. "Think you're better than everyone? Can just shake those hips and drive every guy in here crazy and get away with it?"

"Get. Off. Me." My voice is deathly calm as I dig my elbow into his side to get him off me.

His eyes tighten in anger.

"Ohh. I like a girl that can play rough."

I'm ready to thrust my knee into his balls, but someone comes out of nowhere and grabs him by the shirt collar.

"She said no."

Troy.

I breathe a sigh of relief. I don't think I've ever been so happy to see another person before in my life.

"She was asking for it," the guy slurs.

"No, she wasn't. She told you to stop and you didn't listen. Now get the hell out of here."

Troy drags him to the door and tosses him out.

"Fuck you, man!"

"Don't even think about coming back here. You're not welcome."

Troy's presence is intimidating. It has the few people standing on the porch rushing back inside while others linger to see what's going to happen.

Typical of a college party.

"Don't you have anything better to do?" Troy barks out.

That sends the stragglers running.

"Are you okay?" Troy sidles up to my side, but doesn't come within two feet of me.

"Nothing was going to happen."

Concern laces Troy's face. "That guy was trying

awfully hard."

"I can hold my own."

"You shouldn't have to."

"I appreciate it, Troy. I think I'm going to head home."

There's no way in hell I'm staying out after that.

"Let me walk you home."

"It's okay. You can get back to your party."

Troy takes a tentative step forward. "I don't need to be here. You need me more."

Do I? Now that the adrenaline is starting to seep from my body, I'm tired. I have no doubt that I would've been okay. That guy was drunk enough I could have kicked his ass.

Right?

"Oh my God!" Harper bursts through the front door. "Are you okay?"

"I'm okay."

"Are you sure?" Harper wraps me in her arms. It gives me a moment to settle. "I'll take you home."

Marcus is standing behind her, Troy at his side.

"You stay," I whisper. "Troy will take me home."

"You sure? I don't want to leave you like this."

I pull back, looking her in the eyes. "I promise, I'll be okay. Have fun with Marcus." I turn my attention behind us. "Keep an eye on her."

"I will."

"He will."

Troy and Marcus answer at the same time, causing me and Harper to break out in a fit of giggles. It breaks the tension of the night.

"I'll see you tomorrow." I wink at her and jog down the front porch steps, Troy hot on my heels.

Troy is quiet next to me as we head in the direction of my place. The pointy tips of my heels clack on the sidewalk. It gives me something to focus on other than the warm presence of the man next to me.

"Thank you."

"You don't have to thank me."

"Still. I appreciate what you did."

Troy stuffs his hands in his shorts pockets. "He had no right to do that to you. No person does."

Huh. That surprises me.

Growing up, all I heard was how bad Derek Hollins was because of how he treated my dad while playing. I never thought to question it. Like the sky is blue, the Hollins family was bad news.

Until now.

Troy came to my rescue without thought. Not many people would do that. At a college party, most people are too drunk or busy hooking up to realize what's going on around them.

I'm glad I didn't have to use my skills tonight.

"This is why I don't like coming to parties."

"Because of dicks like him?"

I nod. "I don't mind a party every now and then with Harper, but they're not my thing. Harper wanted to see Marcus, so I agreed to come. We don't let each other go to parties by ourselves."

Campus is buzzing with activity as we cut through the quad. It didn't get late enough for us to be the only ones out. People are still hanging out in the warm evening.

"You're a good friend."

"Am I though?"

The thought of saying no to Troy the other day comes to mind. It makes me feel like a terrible person now. He stepped up for me tonight, and I couldn't do the same.

My building comes into view. I'm ready to take a shower and sleep this night off.

"Thank you, Troy. I really appreciate it."

He follows me up onto the steps as I fish out my keys from my purse and open the door.

"You'll be okay from here?" Troy moves down a step. At this level, his eyes meet mine head-on.

The brown depths would be so easy to get swept away in.

If you were into that kind of thing.

Which I'm not. At all.

"Yeah."

"Good night, Angie." He dips his head and then jogs down the last of the stairs.

"Troy, wait."

I make a split-second decision.

"Yeah?" He turns around, an easy smile on his face.

"I'll help you."

"Come again?"

"I said I'll help you. With astronomy and calculus."

"You don't have to just because I helped you."

"I know. But I want to."

"Are you sure?"

I nod. "Yes. But no one can know."

"Okay."

"I mean it. Nobody."

"It'll be our secret." He mimes zipping his lips.

"Give me your phone."

He unlocks it and passes it over. I open the contacts and drop my number into his. "Text me."

"Thanks, Angie." He gives me one final look before he disappears back into the night.

This night took a turn I never expected. I can't *not* help Troy now. After he came to my defense, it's the least I can do.

I only hope it's not the biggest mistake of my life.

Chapter Six

ANGIE

"Are you sure about this?" Harper asks me, not for the first time.

"Yes, I'm sure."

Even though I'm absolutely *not* sure. I've gone over this about a thousand different ways in my head. Troy was there for me in my time of need, so how can I say no to him now? Every voice in my head is screaming at me that this is a bad idea. That somehow my dads will find out and they'll be more angry than I've ever seen.

They can't really be that mad if I'm only tutoring him, right?

At least I hope.

"Well, good luck." Harper smacks my leg. "I'm going over to see Marcus."

I stow my laptop in my bag and turn to face her. "Things seem to be going well with him."

A dreamy look washes over her face. "They are. He's so hot."

"Is that the only thing you like about him—his looks?"

"As if," she says on a laugh. "There's something

different about him. He's not like the other guys I've dated."

"I've heard that one before." Usually when I'm picking her up off the floor when they break her heart.

"Hey! He really is."

"As long as he's good to you, you know that's all I care about." And from what I've seen, he is. I got to know him a little bit when we got drinks. He seems smitten with her. I'm cautious for my friend. I don't want to see her get her hopes up for some guy to ghost her.

I'm protective of the people I love and don't want anything bad happening to them.

"Enough about me. Go meet Troy and try not to stress."

"Bye, Harper."

I wave after her as she leaves my room. She knows me too well. Because all I've done is worry since I told Troy last night that I would help him.

I'm the good girl. The one that always does what she's told. I never step a toe out of line. I've never had a reason to. Being the rebel or drinking in high school didn't interest me.

Maybe this is my way of rebelling. By helping the person I'm not supposed to be helping.

It's the thought that plagues me as I walk across campus to the library.

I told Troy exactly where to meet me and that's where I find him.

"It bodes well for you that you're already here." I keep my voice light as I drop into the seat beside him.

"Didn't want you to quit on me the first day."

"I wouldn't do that." I tuck a stray piece of hair behind my ear and look at him.

The SDU hockey T-shirt he's wearing stretches across

his chest. His hair is damp, so it's likely that he just came from practice. Brown eyes are playful as they study me.

I wonder what he's thinking. Am I as big of an unknown to him as he is to me? Does he hate my family as much as my family hates his?

"Good." Troy's the first to break our staredown. "What do you want to start with?"

I pull his book toward me, not really seeing which one it is. "What are your classes looking like?"

"We have that astronomy test coming up soon, and I am already lost in that class."

"Then we'll start there."

"How about this book then?" Troy's voice is light as he passes over the correct book. Looking down, I have his calculus book in hand.

"Might be helpful."

"Looks like I might be teaching you something too."

I ignore him. "What are you struggling with the most and we'll start there."

"Uhh…" Troy scrubs a hand over his neck. "Everything?"

I stare at him. He's got a sheepish look on his face. "Do you even like astronomy?"

"No."

"Then why'd you take the class?"

"Because the guys on the team said it'd be an easy A. But I can't figure out how to calculate how far away a black hole is to save my life."

Dropping a hand on his forearm, I open the textbook in front of us. "It's okay. That's what I'm here for."

"I know this is hard for you." Troy drops his hand on top of mine. I ignore how good it feels. How the warmth spreads through me. "I'm only asking for help with classes. Nothing else. Only studying."

"Studying only."

Now if only I can tell my body to get the memo. I haven't reacted to someone like that in years. Or ever, if I'm being honest. My high school boyfriend was more of an infatuation than anything.

"Okay. So how the hell do I identify a black hole?"

I laugh, getting back to the matter at hand. "There's a few different ways to go about black holes."

Flipping open the book, I find the chapter we need. Since we're not that far into the semester, we haven't covered too much material. But the professor we share moves at warp speed. Professor Craig's goal always seems to be to cover the entire book in half the semester.

I walk him through the basics to help with the building blocks. It's how I always start my tutoring sessions. No sense in diving into the deep end if the student doesn't have an understanding of what I'm reviewing.

And based on the way Troy's eyes are glazing over, I'm losing him. "Is any of this making sense?"

"Kind of? All the numbers get jumbled together, and I don't know what I'm actually looking at. Sorry."

I shake my head at him. "Don't be sorry. I'll make sure you understand this before we leave today."

"How long are you planning on being here?"

"Hey now. That means you are doubting my abilities to teach you."

"Well, Professor Craig can't do it, and he has a doctorate."

I roll my eyes. "He really does love talking about that any chance he can get."

"Maybe if he talks about that less, he could teach me more."

"Then you wouldn't be here with me."

Troy drops his elbow on the table and rests his cheek on his fist. "Wouldn't that be better for you then?"

"No." And I mean it. "I like helping people. And I want to help you, Troy; I really do."

"I appreciate it." Troy pulls his book back to him. "Now, tell me this again."

I do as he asks. Even if I have to stay here all afternoon with him and go over it a hundred times, I'll stay here until he gets it right.

It's the fifth time that I'm walking him through the right equation that I see the light click in his eyes.

"Wait. So I use this number here and divide it by this one?" He points to the correct two numbers.

"Yes! That's it!" My voice echoes in the quiet study room we're in. "That's exactly how you do it."

"It seems so easy now." Troy finds another equation in the practice problems and completes it without my help this time. "Is that right?"

I check his math and see that it's correct. "That's right. Great job."

"God, I feel like an idiot for not realizing how easy this was before now."

"Sometimes it just takes the right person to explain it in a way that makes sense."

He nods. "Yeah. I can use this to rewrite my paper considering it's all about black holes."

"That's great. Do you want to review that while we're here?"

"Can we?" There's a trepidation in his voice. I hate that I put it there. My unwillingness to help him the first time shows.

I hate myself a little more for it.

"Let's do it. I have all afternoon."

I walk Troy through his paper, pointing out areas to

improve and things he got right. I can see his confidence building as he makes notes.

Troy drops his pen, staring over at me. His brown eyes are assessing.

"You're really good at this, Angie."

"My pops is a math teacher. I enjoy helping people like this."

"My dad was a high school football coach."

"Really?" That surprises me.

"Didn't have that in your book of knowledge about the Hollins family?"

"As much as my dad talks, some things I didn't think were necessary for me to listen to."

"Like about my family?"

I nod. "I'm learning I also need to form my own opinions."

"So you're forming your own about me then?"

"I'm learning a lot about you. Things I like."

"See? I can teach you a thing or two too, Angie." Troy gives me a winning smile. One that I have to do my best to ignore so the feelings in my belly don't overtake me.

One thing I'm learning about Troy?

I like him. My opinion of him was based solely on what my dad told me about Troy's dad. All I knew about Derek Hollins was what a dirty player he was and how he treated my dad. I never heard what he did when he suddenly disappeared from the league.

Troy was starting out in the negative with me.

Derek Hollins's son? No.

Hockey player? No way. Not ever.

In my mind, there was no redemption for him. Troy has shown me otherwise.

He's more than a hockey player. From what I've seen,

he's nothing like his dad. Or maybe his dad has changed. I don't know.

Because I now realize I know very little about him or his family.

But I've also realized that's something I want to learn.

I need to get this study session back on track.

"How about we go back to me teaching you?"

"What, don't like being in the hot seat?"

"Am I that obvious?" I don't look at him, a blush creeping up my cheeks.

"Only a little."

"In that case, do these five problems and I'll check your work."

He chuckles as he pulls his notebook toward him.

I'm finding Troy's an easy guy to like. Even when he's struggling with school, there's a lightness to his personality. He's dedicated to the hockey team by the way he's making his studies a priority. Even when he could coast and let some student do the work for him.

As our time winds down today, I'm finding I'm excited to see him again. Want to work with him again.

I don't want to admit it, but I have a crush on Troy Hollins.

What am I going to do about it now?

Chapter Seven

TROY

"Can you break it down in hockey terms?"

"Hockey terms?" Angie looks at me like I've lost my mind. I know she's frustrated with me because I'm not understanding it.

We met at the food court between classes today. Her half-eaten sandwich sits between us by the remains of my own lunch. It's loud in here, making it hard to think. It's the only place we could meet before our next class.

We're tucked away in a back corner behind a pillar covered in flyers. It gives us privacy so no one bothers us.

I'd hate for people to see how far behind I am in studying.

"Yeah. It might be easier to understand if I can think of it in hockey terms."

"Calculus doesn't equate to hockey."

I point at her. "That you know of."

"Troy…" Exasperation laces her tone. Yup, she's going to drop me. I'll get cut from the team if I'm not careful.

"Okay, fine. Not hockey terms. But there has to be a way to understand derivatives."

"Let me try again."

I try to keep my own frustrations at bay. Who the fuck needs calculus? It's a freshman level class, but I waited too long to take it and have to cram it in now.

I hate that my entire future hangs on something that I should have taken my freshman year. So much for coasting my senior year.

This is the third time I've met up with Angie to study now. Her help on the astronomy paper helped me get a C. I can't stop there, though. Now my focus has shifted back to calculus. Then it'll have to go back to astronomy.

A never-ending cycle that I hate.

"Wait, stop." I cover her hand with mine. It's warm. Soft. Completely enveloped by my much larger hand. Something I like.

"It's the slope there that I need to be focusing on, yeah?"

"Yes! That's it exactly."

"Oh, thank fuck." I slump back into my chair. For once, I don't feel like an idiot.

"I told you you'd get it."

"Admit it, you're thinking I'm some dumb jock that was hopeless."

"I did not. Not ever." Angie's voice is firm. I like the confidence she has in me.

"Well, I'm glad you don't think I'm some idiot hockey player."

"I have other opinions about hockey, but you're not an idiot."

I lean over my books, studying Angie. I haven't missed her subtle digs about hockey. I feel like it's part of why she doesn't like me.

"Why do you hate hockey players so much?"

"I do not hate hockey players."

"You totally do. It's not just me. I know why you hated me."

"I d—"

I hold up a hand, cutting her off. "And don't say you don't. I know you do."

Angie stares down at her hands, fidgeting on the table between us. It's like she's deciding what she wants to tell me. The truth or another lie?

"It was my high school boyfriend. He played for the hockey team."

Looking up at me, Angie's eyes are closed off. For as much as she keeps her emotions close to the vest, her eyes usually give her away. But now, I can't get a read on her.

"I started dating him when I was a freshman. He was a sophomore and was a starter for the varsity team."

"He sounds like a dick."

That gets a laugh out of her. "He was. Cocky as all hell. I still don't know what I saw in him. I think I got swept up in how popular he was."

"Like any high school romance."

"If you can call it that. More like an infatuation."

"So what happened?" I ask.

Angie cringes. "He broke up with me before he left for college. Said he didn't want to be tied down and needed to play the field."

"What a dick. Does he still play?"

She nods. "Kyle Tanner."

"The star from Boston?" My jaw drops. Damn. Angie wasn't kidding when she said he was a dick.

"One and the same."

"He is a fucking douchebag. I played with him at a hockey camp one summer. Slept with anything on legs."

"Turns out he was sleeping with half the school while we were together. I was so heartbroken when he dumped me then I find that out? He made me feel like the biggest idiot. I couldn't believe how stupid I was. I should've known better."

I shake my head. "No, guys like that are good at deceiving people. They tell you exactly what you want to hear to make it okay."

"Is that from your own experience?"

"Fuck no. If there's one thing my dad taught me, it's to respect women."

"He did?" Her tone is questioning.

"He's not the person you think he is. He taught me to be better than he was."

"Still,"—Angie straightens—"it turned me off hockey."

I whistle. "Wow. I'm sorry. That really sucks. Hockey is the greatest sport out there."

"Whatever you say, Troy."

"But you know that's not a thing of all hockey players, right?"

Angie rolls her eyes. "Logically? Yes. But whatever love I had for the game, he took with him to Boston."

"Is it bad that I hate him?"

"You totally can." Angie laughs. "I hate him too."

I know we play Boston this season. And even though he is a year older than I am, he was a redshirt, which means I'll play against him. I want to lay that asshole out for what he did to Angie. I don't know how anyone could ever cheat on this woman.

She's letting me in. Little by little. Angie deserves way better than that guy. She will go out of her way to help anyone. Even me. It might've taken her awhile to get there, but she did.

"I'm surprised you're even talking to me right now."

"So you see why I hate hockey players now."

"Correction, one hockey player. You like me, right?"

"Aren't you getting ahead of yourself?" Angie leans across the table.

"That wasn't a no."

"You're wearing me down, I guess."

"I'm sure my smarts are the biggest draw."

"Wouldn't you like to know?"

I like this playful side of Angie. She's not as serious as I first thought. Definitely not as uptight. I want to keep spending this time with her. If I'm learning something while we're at it, even better.

But I want more. I want to show Angie that not all hockey players are like Kyle. God, I even hate his name. I want to smash the guy's face in. But later. I'll get my chance to.

"Come to our game this weekend. Let me show you how good hockey can be."

"I don't know."

"Please." I'm not above begging to get her to the game. "You'll be my good luck charm."

"You're not supposed to have those," Angie points out. "It's actually bad luck."

"Okay, fine. But I'd like you to come. See what it's like when I'm playing."

Her face twists up, like she's debating it. I don't say a word. Knowing my luck, I'll say the wrong thing and she won't come.

"You'll get your calc test score before the game?"

"Should have it Friday."

She shoves my book toward me. "Study. Get a B and I'll be there."

"Does a B- count?"

"I'll allow it."
"Then a B- it'll be. You'll see."
Anything to get Angie to a game.

Chapter Eight

TROY

ANGIE

So?

TROY

So what?

<<eye roll emoji>> what did you get?!

B+ <<picture of test score>>.

TROY! That is amazing!!

You know what that means?

I know...

Don't sound so excited, Ang

I'm mustering the enthusiasm as we speak

You should be more excited getting to see me play :)

I hear Marcus is a really good player. Maybe I should wear his jersey?

> Aren't you something…

> You like it, admit it

> Oh, I do. And now I have to get ready to make sure I play my best tonight

> Show-off

> For you? Yeah

"How many times are you going to wrap your stick?" Randy chucks a sock at my head.

"Don't mess with superstition."

"Aren't you the one telling me not to believe in that stuff?"

I pull the tape off my stick and start over. It helps keep the edge off since I know Angie will be at the game tonight.

We've got an easy workout this afternoon before dinner and our game.

"It's only crazy if it doesn't work."

I wrap the red tape around the end of my stick. It's something I've been doing since high school. Takes the nervous edge off that I always get before games.

No matter how long I've been playing, that feeling never goes away. It's only gotten worse as the stakes get bigger.

I know there are scouts here tonight. I should be wanting to impress them, but it's not them I'm focused on.

I'm focused on Angie. Wanting to impress her and score a hat trick tonight.

"Hollins. My office. Now," Coach Morris barks out.

"Ooh. Are you in trouble?" Randy sings from his stall.

"Fuck off." I flip him off as I head for Coach's office.

Not that I have any clue what I did. Or didn't do for that matter. We've already gone over the game plan tonight for playing Cal U.

They haven't won a game all season, so this should be an easy win.

At least I'm hoping it will be.

"You wanted to see me?" I stick my head into his office and wait for him to wave me in.

"How are your classes coming along this semester?"

"Classes?"

Unless I tanked another exam that I didn't realize since I've been so focused on my two worst subjects.

"I got an email from Professor Smith."

"What did it say?" I try to swallow around the sudden dryness coating my mouth. It couldn't be that bad, especially since I did so well on the last test.

"He says you've improved immensely since the start of the semester."

"Shit. Really?"

Coach nods. "As you know, I keep in regular contact with all of your professors to make sure you're maintaining the academic standards I've come to expect from my players."

"I've been trying. I don't take my starting position lightly. Classes were not what I was expecting this semester." I scrub at my jaw. No sense in lying to him. Coach Morris has a bullshit radar detector.

"Expected to coast your final year?"

I shake my head. "Not at all."

"Good. I expect you to keep up the hard work. I don't want to lose my captain this far into the season."

"I don't plan on it, Coach."

"That's what I like to hear. I'll see you on the ice."

The nerves from being called into his office lessen, as the nerves for the game grow. Marcus is waiting for me by my stall as I grab my stick and finish taping it up.

"What'd Coach want?" He takes a swig from his water bottle.

"To tell me Professor Smith says how I've improved this semester."

"Damn, way to go, Gladiator."

I toss the roll of tape into my locker and grab a towel to hit the training room. "I thought I was about to be demoted."

"Nah. We couldn't survive without you."

Marcus and I stick together all afternoon through our workout and dinner, shooting the shit and helping the lowerclassmen with their workouts.

By the time we're suiting up for the game, an excited energy is flowing through me. I follow Marcus out of the locker room and into the tunnel that will lead us to the ice. I can hear people above us now. It's going to be loud tonight.

Cal U has always been one of our rivals. Even though they haven't been playing well this season, it's going to be a fight.

Their fans will show up for the game tonight.

"You think Angie is coming to the game with Harper tonight?"

"She said she was."

And it makes me want to play better for her.

"I think she likes you."

I roll my eyes at him. "You sound like a high schooler."

Marcus elbows me in the side. It does nothing since I'm wearing my gear. He pulls his shield down and steps out onto the ice. "Dude, *you're* acting like a high schooler who likes someone but doesn't want to admit it."

"Am not!" I shout after him.

It's no use. He's off to our end of the rink to start warm-ups.

Fucker.

I like Angie. I know I do. It doesn't make me a high schooler by wanting to hear that she likes me back.

Except…

Damn it.

It's exactly how I feel. I invited Angie to the game tonight, and I honestly have no idea if she'll come.

I skate through warm-ups without much thought. My muscles are loose as I shoot pucks toward the net. A few misses, but the vast majority of them go in.

It's a sea of red as I take in the home crowd. It's packed. Wall-to-wall people with the student section now cheering us on. Loudly. People are banging on the glass as we continue our warm-ups. Highlight reels play on the TVs that hang above the ice.

I love the energy our home crowd brings. It's one of my favorite parts of the game. Sometimes, it gives me chills. I can't believe I get to play the sport I love at this level.

And hopefully continue on to the pros.

Coach calls for us all to head into the locker room, and I fist-bump every guy as they skate off the ice.

The atmosphere in here is electric. The team is ready. Music is blasting from a speaker to pump the team up. Everyone is fired up and ready to get out there on the ice.

"Alright, men," Coach Morris calls out to us. "Cal U hasn't won a game yet, but it doesn't mean we take this game any less seriously than others. I want you to go out there tonight and show them what Sand Shark hockey is all about. Play hard. Play strong and let's go out there and take the win!"

"Sand Sharks on three! One, two three…" Randy trails off and we all echo him.

The entire team skates onto the ice as one. Lights are flashing as the crowd is screaming. I love the energy. I feed off it. It spurs me on to play better.

Both teams gather at their respective lines as the anthem starts to play. It's one of the few times before the game that I can shut everything out and focus on the team we're playing.

Cal U's top scorer went out in their first game, and they've struggled finding their footing ever since. They have a weak defense, and I'm hoping I can take advantage of it tonight.

By the time I look up, we're ready to start the game.

"Kick ass out there, Gladiator."

Marcus holds his gloved fist out for me.

"Kick ass, Wizard."

Skating to center ice, I'm ready for the puck drop. The kid standing across from me has a cocky grin on his face. I wonder if I looked like that back in the day. Now, I'm all business as I get ready for the game to start.

The whistle blows and the puck is dropped. I easily snatch the puck from the guy and send it flying across the ice to Marcus, who passes it to Randy before it gets shot back to me.

We're a well-oiled machine, moving across the ice. Cal U's defense isn't ready for us as I deke the defenseman and easily put the puck in the back of the net.

The stands erupt.

"Holy shit, you motherfucker!" Randy glides over to me and jumps onto me. "I don't think we've ever scored that fast before!"

Looking at the time clock, nine seconds have ticked by.

"It's going to be a long game for them." Marcus is positively giddy as he slaps me on the helmet as we head back for the ensuing face-off.

"Don't get cocky now," I tell the two of them. A fast start doesn't mean anything when we still have the entire game left to play.

"Keep playing like that and I will be."

I roll my eyes at Randy and take the face-off. The poor kid doesn't look quite so cocky anymore. He's not fast, and I take the puck out from under him. This time, we're not as lucky. Cal U's defense is ready for us and blocks what could have been an easy pass from Randy to me.

Our guys are ready at the other end of the ice. We have one of the best defenses in the country, and they easily block Cal U from getting anywhere close to our goalie.

Taking the puck back toward their end of the ice, Marcus slides into position as I pass the puck off. Randy follows behind, blocking their defenseman so Marcus can take the shot on goal.

The lamp lights up behind the goalie.

2-0 Sand Sharks.

"Fuck yeah!" I congratulate Marcus on another easy goal.

"Wanna save one for me, boys?" Randy asks.

"Gotta take your own shots, Randy," Marcus tells him.

Coach calls for a line change before play resumes. Finding my spot on the bench, I look around the crowd.

Electric. That's the only way to describe it. There's no way I could find Angie in here right now. But I'm hoping she's here.

And it's that thought that carries me through the rest of the game.

7-2. An easy win if there ever was one.

"Great win, boys! A hat trick from our captain and an assist? Hell of a game, Hollins."

"Thanks, Coach."

"Practice is canceled tomorrow. Take the day, rest up, and I'll see you all on Monday."

Thank God. I could use a rest day. Between practice and studying, I have no life.

"Anyone down to party tonight?" Randy asks. "I'll pick up some kegs on the way home."

"You know it!" Isaac tells him. "You up for it, Gladiator?"

"Gotta celebrate a win," I agree, even though I know I'll make it an early night.

I take a quick shower, wanting to go out and see if I can find Angie.

As I leave the locker room, Cal U is walking out of the visitors' locker room and heading to their buses.

"Hey." I call over their player who'd been trying to keep up with us all night.

"Me?" He looks around, like he's trying to gauge who I'm talking to.

"Yeah. C'mere." I wave him over. His bag looks like it might swallow him whole. *Was I that small when I was just starting out?* "What's your name?"

"Austin Lamontagne."

"Austin. You played hard tonight."

"Don't have much to show for it," he mutters. There's not a trace of the cockiness from when we started the game.

"You scored. That's a positive."

"You annihilated us. Not much to be positive about."

"Are you a freshman?" I ask.

He nods. "I got bumped up to the starting line because two of the guys got busted for cheating."

"Shit. No wonder it's been a hard season."

"Yeah. No one is really happy with how things are going."

I smack him on the arm. "Don't get discouraged. You have four years ahead of you. A lot can happen during that time."

"I'm trying not to think that far ahead. I'd love to play in the NHL, but I don't know if I'm good enough."

"Look, it was one loss—"

"After another after another after another," he interjects. "Hard to come back from."

"I scored on my own team my freshman year."

"You did?" That gets his attention.

I nod. "Worst fucking feeling in the world. Trust me, I know. But it gets better."

"Yeah, okay." Austin perks up a bit. "Hey, thanks. I appreciate it."

"Don't sweat it. Hopefully I'll see you around."

"Thanks, Troy!"

He heads out to where I know the team buses are undoubtedly waiting for him.

"That was nice of you."

A warm voice has me spinning on my heel.

Angie.

She's wearing an SDU hockey sweatshirt, red knit cap, leggings, and white tennis shoes. Her brown hair is flowing around her shoulders, and her cheeks are pink from the cold.

I didn't think Angie could get any more sexy, but she is. She looks fucking gorgeous.

"You saw that?"

Angie pushes off the cinderblock wall she's leaning against and walks over to me. Guys are still filtering out of the locker room. Grabbing her elbow, I guide her to a quiet alcove.

"I did." A small smile plays on her lips. "It was really nice of you."

"Kid's got talent." I brush it off. "It's what anyone would have done."

She shakes her head. "I don't think a lot of people would do something like that. Especially on the opposing team."

"No sense in crushing his dreams. He's good."

"Good enough to beat you?"

"Hey now!" I laugh. "Maybe not that good."

Angie nods at me, taking me in. "Getting a little cocky there, Troy."

"Not cocky if I can back it up."

"You played well tonight," Angie confirms.

"You think so?" I take a step closer to her. Her eyes make a slow perusal over me as they travel over my body to meet my gaze.

"You did. Coming from someone who doesn't care about hockey, I can say you are a great player."

I want to preen like a damn peacock under her praise. Even though I hoped she was here tonight, no matter how much I kept telling myself to play for myself, I was playing for her. Not even the scouts in the crowd could beat out wanting to impress her.

"Thanks, Ang. That means a lot coming from you."

"You might turn me into a hockey fan yet."

"One game wasn't enough?"

"Score another hat trick and then we'll see."

"You know what they do after a hat trick, right?"

"What's that?" Angie crosses her arms over her chest. The small movement pushes her against me. It's the slightest touch but one that sends heat barreling through me.

Fuck. I really should not be having this reaction to her.

"You get a hat." I tug on the white pom-pom that sits on top of her hat.

"And you want mine?"

"It's all part of the game."

There's a gleam in Angie's eyes. "Well, I guess if it's part of the game…"

She pulls it off her head and shoves it down over mine. The thing is a lot smaller on my head, but the warmth from her more than makes up for it.

"How do I look?" I smile down at her.

"There's no way that can be comfortable." She's laughing at me. "I'm taking it back."

"No way!" I dodge out of her way. "If I don't score another hat trick in the next game, I'll give it back."

"So this is a back and forth now?"

"I'm making it so," I declare. "If it gets you to another game…"

Angie studies me. I shouldn't be hanging on to her every word, but I am. I want more with her. More than she's likely willing to give me right now. But I'll take every crumb she throws my way.

"Then I guess you better score then." She bounds off down the tunnel toward the exit without another word.

And maybe I'll score with her.

Chapter Nine

"Where are you running off to?"

I pull the T-shirt over my head and glance over at Marcus.

"Study session today."

He gives me a cursory glance. "You've been studying a lot lately."

"Because if I don't, I'm going to fail and then get kicked off the hockey team."

"Yeah, but I feel like I haven't seen you in weeks."

"Wizard, we live together and play together. I see you every day."

He waves me off. "You know what I mean. We haven't hung out together in ages."

"Aww, are you feeling neglected?" I rub his still-damp hair from the shower.

"Fuck off."

"You have Harper. Don't act like you've been around."

Marcus's eyes glaze over. No doubt he's thinking about her. If he's not at hockey practice, he's spending time with her. I've never seen the guy so loved up.

"It's our senior year. We should at least see each other more than when required."

"Then you want to go out tonight?" I ask him, throwing everything in my gym bag to take home. "I hear the football team is having a party."

"Harper and I were supposed to go out, but maybe all four of us could?"

Going out with Angie? So far, the only thing we've done together is study. Is going to a party together considered a date?

"I'll ask her, but no promises."

"Will you come if she doesn't want to go?" Marcus stands, and we head out of the locker room, waving goodbye to the other guys.

"And be a third wheel? Fuck that."

"Ouch. I see where I stand."

"Marcus." I drop my arm around his shoulders and pull him toward me. "It's where I stand. And I'm totally fine with it."

"Get off me, asshole." His tone is playful. "Where do *you* stand with Angie?"

"She's my tutor."

"And?"

"And what? That's it."

Marcus shakes his head at me. "Would you be studying this much with your tutor if it were anyone *but* Angie?"

"Yes," I lie.

I'd probably be doing more studying on my own if I'm honest. There's something about Angie that makes me want to be around her. Was she standoffish at first? Yes. But now that I've gotten to know her, there's more to her.

She's kind. Funny. Sweet. Caring.

And so damn sexy, it drives me crazy that I can't be with her like that.

Angie Brooks-Young is the forbidden fruit. One I wouldn't mind sinking my teeth into. If only for one taste.

One taste would be dangerous. Because I'd become addicted to her.

"Keep telling yourself that, Gladiator." Marcus elbows me in the side. "Text me if you're coming tonight."

I nod at him. "See ya, man."

Heading in the opposite direction, I go to the food court to pick up lunch for Angie and me before meeting her at a quiet park near campus. For a bright and sunny fall day in San Diego, it's quiet. Maybe because it's the middle of the week, but Angie is the only one on this side of the park.

Her books are spread out on the table as she writes away in her notebook.

I don't know why I find her studying so hot, but I do. Maybe it's the dedication to her work—something I've never had, but I like that in her. She's passionate about learning the way I am about hockey. It's probably why we get along so well.

"Hey, Troy." Her head pops up, a smile on her face.

"Hey." I drop the bag of sandwiches on the table and sit across from her. "I brought us lunch."

"Thank God. I'm starving."

"Glad I can help." I reach into the brown paper bag and hand hers over. "Turkey and avocado on wheat."

She eyes me with a mix of awe and curiosity. "How do you already know my sandwich order?"

"You get the same thing every time we've been together. It's not hard."

"Most guys wouldn't notice things like that."

"It's easy to notice things about you, Angie."

There's a flicker of something that passes across her face, but it's gone before I can figure out what it is.

"How was your psych test yesterday?" Angie changes the subject, biting into her sandwich.

"Not too bad. Got a B+."

"Hey, that's great!" Angie's face widens with delight. I like that she checks in with me on all my classes, not just the ones she's helping me with.

"Pretty sad that a B+ is great for me."

"Hey, psych is hard. It takes time to learn things."

I shake my head. "I don't believe you."

"I struggled a lot in middle school. The only reason I got better is because my pops is a math teacher."

"My dad was friends with the math teacher at our school, so he helped me a lot in high school. Also doubled as the hockey coach."

"He was?" Shock colors her expression now. "I'm trying to imagine my pops as a hockey coach and I just can't picture it."

I laugh. "Yeah, he wasn't what you would picture a hockey coach to be."

Angie sets her lunch aside, leaning across the table. "Okay, I know your dad coached high school football. How in the world—"

"Did I end up playing hockey?" I cut her off.

"Yes. They are so different. I imagine your dad wanted you to follow in his footsteps…play for Vegas?"

The silence between the two of us is awkward. We both know what my dad did when he played for Vegas. No doubt her dad told her all the terrible things he did.

My dad's side is different. I know the person he is. The kind, loving, caring, and gentle man he is now. There's not a bad bone in his body. I hate that this is the impression she has of him. He's one of the most important people in my life, and I'll do anything to defend him.

But Angie would do the same for her dad.

"Our school was lucky enough to have a hockey team," I tell her. "My dad was good friends with the coach because they taught together. We'd go to the games together when I was little and I loved it. I loved how fast they could skate backward. Thought it was the coolest thing at that age."

"It is impressive what you can do on two tiny blades."

"The coach helped me out and gave me lessons and there was no turning back after that. Nothing could get me off the ice."

Angie rests her chin in her hand, a soft look now on her face. "I can only imagine how cute you were as a kid. Oversized pads and wobbling around the ice."

I laugh, deep and hearty. "I will never introduce you to my mom then. She would be breaking out all the home videos of me and my sister."

"Your sister plays too?"

I nod. "She's on the national team."

"Wow. I'm impressed. I was never good at sports."

"You can't have it all, Angie. If you were good at sports too, you'd be a triple threat."

"A triple threat?" Her eyes are glittering.

"Smart, hot, *and* good at sports? It'd be unfair to the world."

"Then maybe I'll need to have you teach me something."

"I'd love to get you in a pair of skates and see how you fare on the ice."

She points her finger at me. "Only if you get an A on your next calc test."

"There's some motivation to study."

"Good. Then get to it." Angie passes the book over to me with the problems she's written out and goes back to her lunch.

It's hard to focus with her sitting right there.

I wasn't lying when I said it'd be good motivation. I want to be someone that Angie can be proud to be seen with. Not another dumb jock.

I shouldn't want that, but I do.

It's why I'm spending so much time studying with her. I want to be around her every minute I can. I had no plans to start dating my senior year. Hockey should be my one and only focus. Well, that and school.

But for a girl like Angie? I'd be willing to break every rule I have to be with her.

If only she would too.

I clear those thoughts from my head, going back to the problems at hand. Ones that she's taught me how to solve.

A cool breeze blows through the park as I finish the problems and pass the notebook back over to her to check them.

I figure now might be as good a time as any to ask her about going out.

"Listen. Marcus and Harper are going to the football party tonight, and I wanted to see if you wanted to go."

"With you?" she asks, crumpling the paper her sandwich was wrapped in and putting it in the bag.

"Yeah. But not like a date or anything," I tack on. I know her rules. Only studying. If she got any whiff that I wanted to ask her out, she'd shoot me down.

She doesn't answer me, going back to look at my work.

"It's okay if you don't want to go. I know you're not much of a partier."

This time, when she looks back up at me, her face is bright.

"I guess I should go since you answered all of the problems correctly."

"No way." I grab it back from her to look and check my own work. "Shit. I did."

"You're smart, Troy. Practice makes perfect, right?"

"It's because of you," I tell her. "I wouldn't have gotten this without you."

"You're doing the hard work." She tucks her hair behind her ear, a blush creeping over her cheeks. God, what I wouldn't give to see more of that.

"Back to the party. You said you guess you should go?"

"As long as it's not a date..." she trails off then adds, "I'll go."

I throw my hands up in defense. "Not a date. Just going out with friends of ours that think I'm ditching them to study."

Angie laughs, loud and sweet. "Harper thinks I'm ditching her to study too!"

"When really the two of them are glued together."

"Harper is halfway in love with him by now."

"So we'll just go and support our friends falling in love. Nothing else."

"Nothing else," she agrees.

Because Marcus and Harper can have that future together. Not us.

Angie is only my tutor. Nothing else.

Even if I want her to be so much more.

Chapter Ten

ANGIE

"Do I look okay?" I ask Harper, not for the first time tonight.

"Why do you care so much? It's not like you're trying to impress anybody, right?" Harper quirks a perfectly manicured brow in my direction.

"I still want to look good."

"Angie, you look hot. Troy won't know what hit him."

I try to quell the rising happiness in me at that statement, but it's hard. Because every time I'm around Troy, this crush keeps becoming something more. These feelings keep growing.

Wiggly ones that keep trying to worm their way into my head and heart.

Tonight, I'm pushing all of that out of my head. Tonight we're going to hang out together with our friends at the football party.

"It's a good thing you have Marcus, because the guys would be all over you."

Harper is stunning. In a black leather miniskirt and a

black bodysuit, she's curled her hair and added a pop of bright pink lipstick. Marcus won't know what hit him.

"Please. You'll be fending off the guys too."

I opted for skinny jeans and a black off-the-shoulder top. Nothing too flashy, but still, an outfit I feel good in.

"More like holding up the wall."

"One of these days, I'll get you out on the dance floor."

"When pigs fly." I laugh.

The street is crowded as students are coming and going from parties. The street is crowded as students are coming and going from parties, but Troy and Marcus are waiting for us at the corner.

And damn, do they both look good.

Harper drops my arm and bounds over to Marcus, laying a smacking kiss on his mouth.

Troy's eyes stay on me. He's wearing jeans, a gray V-neck T-shirt, and a leather jacket. It's nothing major, but he makes it look good.

"Wow, Angie. Can I tell you that you look good?"

"You can."

I preen under his praise. Something I should definitely *not* be doing. Tonight, I want to have fun. I want to do what every other college student does. Maybe get into a little bit of trouble.

The *good kind* of trouble.

"You ready to get going?" Troy throws a thumb over his shoulder.

"Yeah."

"You okay to be going to a party?" The two of us are walking behind Harper and Marcus, who keep stealing kisses from each other.

"Because of last time?"

"Yeah."

"I appreciate you checking in, Troy, but I'm okay."

"Promise?"

"Promise."

I get bumped into Troy from someone running down the street. A steady arm wraps around my shoulders. I make no effort to move.

I like being in his arms.

Too much for my own good.

"Let's party!" Harper turns around, shouting back at us as we enter the house. It's big. Bigger than the hockey house. A staircase wraps around the right side of the house, and a disco ball hangs where a chandelier likely used to hang. A living room packed with people is off to the left, and straight back is a kitchen with more people overflowing into the hall.

We move into the living room where a DJ is blasting the latest rock tune.

"I'll grab us a drink," Troy tells me.

"I'll wait here."

Marcus heads off with him as Harper makes her way back to my side. "You two are looking pretty cozy."

"Stop it."

I don't need Harper getting any ideas in her head.

"You two would make a cute couple."

"Harper, seriously?"

I also don't want her putting any ideas in *my* head. Because it won't happen.

"I'm done, I'm done." She throws her hands up. "I'll just focus on Marcus tonight."

"Who's focusing on me?" Marcus and Troy are back, red Solo cups in hand.

"Me." Harper presses a kiss to his lips before dragging him off to dance. "Let's go, baby."

"Want to dance?" Troy asks.

"Not yet. I need way more liquid courage before that happens."

"You? I bet you have moves, Angie." Troy's eyes make a slow walk up my body. It sends tingles racing through me.

I laugh, sipping on the beer, shaking off the feelings. "More like a turtle flailing around on his back."

"I doubt that."

"You overestimate my skills, Troy."

"Okay." Troy grabs my cup midsip and sets it down on a table behind us. "Now you don't get a say."

"In what?"

Troy rests two hands on my hips, turning me to him. He leans down, his breath a whisper against my ear. "Will you dance with me?"

The way his breath flutters over me has goose bumps erupting all over my skin. There's only one answer. Saying no to Troy never even enters my mind.

Slipping my hand into his, I walk out onto the dance floor.

Bodies are everywhere, pressing the two of us closer together. I run my hands up his broad chest. His hands land on my hips, moving us to the beat.

I've always wondered what Troy felt like. Every time we're together, he wears shirts that cling to his every muscle.

Feeling them now under my fingers? I want to strip his shirt off and see what they feel like without this fabric.

Because muscles he does have. Ones that send dirty thoughts racing through my brain.

Someone bumps into me from behind, and Troy pulls me farther into his space. There's no room between us.

I hate how perfectly I fit with him, like a puzzle piece. I

shouldn't be thinking that, but I am. My hands are moving on their own, clasping his neck.

I want to run my hands through his hair, feel how soft it is.

His eyes widen as they stare down at me. It's like we're the only two people in this crowded house. Troy's gaze doesn't waver. He is only looking at me.

It's an overwhelming feeling being under his stare like this. His eyes hold so much emotion. Emotions that are telling me he wants me.

"You're better than you think," Troy tells me. His lips vibrate against my ear. I want to feel those lips everywhere.

"You make me better."

"Nah. All you, Ang."

I love the way he says my name like that. Like there's a connection between the two of us. A feeling that takes hold in me and won't let go.

I've been feeling it for a while. Every time I'm with Troy, I want to be around him more. He's nothing like I thought he'd be. He's proven that day in and day out.

It was me who started this thing off on the wrong foot. Denying him when he needed my help all because of our families.

I'm done. Done denying myself what I want. Done denying myself him.

I want him to kiss me. I want him to close the small space between us and close his lips over mine.

But he won't.

I told Troy what this thing was between us.

Tutoring. That's it.

Now? Now I want it to be more. And I'm going to have to be the one to take the leap into more.

So be it.

I take what I want. I don't think about the consequences of my actions. I don't weigh the pros and cons of what this might mean.

I press up onto my toes and kiss him. Troy responds immediately.

Soft lips open, giving me command of this kiss. I waste no time sliding my tongue into his mouth. He tastes like the beer he was sipping.

Troy's hands move from my hips to my face, holding me close. It tells me he wants this just as much as I do.

I cling to him tighter. Every thought is zapped from my brain as our tongues tangle. A buzz I've never felt is moving through me as we stand here in the middle of a crowded dance floor and kiss.

And kiss.

And *kiss*.

My toes curl, and heat gathers in my core as Troy tilts my head and changes the angle. My belly swoops, wanting more.

I moan as Troy nips my bottom lip before kissing his way along my jaw.

My body is on overload. I'm feeling too many things. Not enough things.

All because of Troy.

"Angie," he grunts out, tugging my earlobe between his teeth.

"Oh God."

If Troy didn't have a hold on me, I'd melt into a heap on the floor. Instead, I wrap my arms around his shoulders and bring his mouth back to mine.

If this kiss is all the two of us will get, I want it to last.

It's something Troy seems to understand. There's a fire to this kiss that wasn't there a minute ago. Each of us taking and giving as we learn and discover.

Until the music changes and everyone in the room

starts shouting. The SDU fight song plays on the speakers.

"Fucking football team," Troy grumbles.

"What?" My brain is in a kiss-altered state. I couldn't tell you my own name right now, that's how good this kiss was.

"They always play it before they leave for away games."

Ahh. "Explains why there's a party on a Wednesday night."

"Angie…"

"Don't." I cover his mouth with my fingers. "I don't regret this at all, if that's what you're thinking."

His mouth moves into a smile under my hand. "Not what I was going to say. I was going to ask if you wanted to keep doing this."

"Maybe not in the middle of the dance floor."

"Troy. We need to go." Marcus appears next to us.

"What?"

"A few of the guys got busted at a party and we need to go pick them up."

"Are you fucking kidding me?" He groans, dropping his head to my shoulder. "We just got here."

"Do you want half the freshmen to get kicked off the team?" Marcus gives Troy a look that is obvious of the correct answer.

"Sometimes I hate being the captain."

"No you don't." I draw his face back and smile up at him. "You wouldn't be you if you didn't go help."

"Think we can get a raincheck on this?"

I nod. "Raincheck."

I don't know what will happen, but maybe we can continue this thing. Maybe we won't want to after the buzz clears.

I guess we'll see. All I know right now is I want Troy.

Chapter Eleven

ANGIE

"I'm surprised I was able to talk you into going."

"You did not have to talk me into this," I correct Harper.

"That's right. Things seem to be going well with you and Troy."

A blush creeps up my cheeks. I hate how easily my face shows what I'm feeling. Right now it's showing every single thing I'm feeling for Troy.

Just thinking his name has my belly swooping low. It's only been a few weeks since I started tutoring him, but each time we're together, I look forward to it more and more.

It's dangerous, being with him. Every time one of my dads calls, I'm worried I'm going to let it slip. Even if they knew I was tutoring him, they'd flip their lid.

I don't want to be on the receiving end of that. My lips are zipped tight. The only person who knows about this is Harper.

But Harper is too interested in Marcus at the moment to worry about me and Troy.

"You know hockey isn't my thing."

"Hot men crashing into each other on the ice? Hockey butts? Thick thighs? None of that is appealing to you?" Harper's mouth gapes open at me in horror.

"I didn't say it wasn't appealing. You know my history."

She rolls her eyes as we fight through the crowds to find seats in the stands. SDU's hockey team is the most popular team on campus, so the fundraiser event to watch their practice is one everyone wants to attend. Probably for all the reasons Harper listed and then some.

"Troy isn't convincing you otherwise?"

"He might be."

She got me here tonight without a fight. We find two open seats and make our way down the row. The team is already on the ice, showcasing their skills for the adoring public.

My eyes lock on to him on the ice.

He's a force to be reckoned with. A powerful player if I've ever seen one. It's like he's one with his stick and the puck.

Watching the play set up around him is mesmerizing. Even though it's only practice, they're taking it seriously. Faking out the defenseman, it's him and the winger. He passes the puck off to Marcus who slips it past the waiting goalie.

Cheers ring out around the arena.

"Marcus scoring is hot," Harper tells me. "He's so getting lucky tonight."

"Harper!"

"What? I'm not going to lie. Hockey turns me on."

I roll my eyes. "Of course it does."

Troy slams someone into the boards and steals the puck from them. From there, it's another easy goal.

I know it's not like this in games, but it looked easy at the game I was at. A hat trick? I know that's hard to get.

Harper isn't wrong though. Watching someone that is competent at their sport *is* hot.

"Chin up there, Angie." Harper taps my chin. "You wouldn't want people to know you like hockey."

I clamp my mouth shut, not sure when it dropped in awe. At least, I hope that was it. I don't need to be seen drooling over Troy.

"You're the one that's ogling Marcus."

Harper wraps an arm around my shoulder, pulling me into her side. "And you're just like the rest of us, Angela. Hot for hockey players."

"Stop it. I am not." I try to shove her off me, but she doesn't let up.

"It's okay to admit that you like him."

Blue eyes pierce mine.

"Never going to happen."

"You are too stubborn for your own good, you know that, right?"

I laugh. "Am not."

"I'll just ask Troy after practice." She gives me a haughty smile.

"You know why it'll never happen."

"But it could," she corrects me.

"Nope, not a chance. I can't even entertain that thought."

"It's like you're Romeo and Juliet."

"They have nothing on feuding football families."

Harper laughs. "Except Troy plays hockey."

"Same difference."

Leaning forward, Harper keeps her eyes on the ice. Marcus has the puck now. "I wouldn't be opposed to Marcus playing football."

I laugh. "So we can interchange him with any other athlete and you'd be fine?"

She gasps at me. "Hell no. It's all Marcus."

A dreamy look washes over her face. God. I hope I don't look like that when I think of Troy.

Which I don't.

Except when I'm working on tutoring plans. That's it.

The puck is stolen from Marcus but Troy gets it back just as easily. This time, the goalie blocks the shot and a whistle is blown for a time-out.

"They are really good," I confess.

"Wow. How much did that hurt to say?"

"I don't know why I'm friends with you."

"I'm a delight."

"A delightful pain in my ass," I mutter back.

She smirks at me, and we both watch the rest of practice in a contented silence, commenting every so often on a good play.

The team gathers at center ice around Troy. He's no doubt hyping them up after a great practice. They all shout "Sand Sharks" before skating off the ice. Troy lingers on the mascot on the rink, gaze searching the stands.

It has my breath catching and my heart banging around in my chest when his eyes rake over me. He can't see me from where he is, but it feels like he can. Especially when a smile curls his lips.

It's not for me. It's not for me. It's not for me.

No matter how many times I tell myself that, I really *want* his smile to be for me.

Damn it.

I'm letting my feelings take over. My head isn't in control right now. My heart is. It's what led me to kiss him. What led me to come here today.

What's controlling every decision I make about Troy now.

I can't help it.

"C'mon. I told Marcus we'd meet him in the lobby." Harper's voice tugs me from my wayward thoughts.

Nerves burble in my stomach. I'm anxious to see him. I didn't tell him I was coming today. I hope like hell he's happy to see me.

We're in his territory today.

I swallow down the nerves the best I can and follow her like a lost puppy.

Harper and I are waiting by the doors when the team starts filtering out. People are fawning all over the guys like they're rock stars.

This is why I have such issues with hockey players. Any athletes, really. Kyle loved this attention. He fed off it. Ate up every ounce of it.

He couldn't have cared less about me by the time we broke up.

After that, I never went out with a player again. I didn't want to deal with this.

Seeing Troy walk out of the locker room is bringing back a lot of bad memories for me. Instead of him reveling in it, his eyes spot me and he makes a beeline my way.

"Hey. You came." He sounds surprised. "I didn't think you would."

"You looked really good out there," I tell him.

Marcus comes over to us and whisks Harper up into his arms. Those two are oblivious to everyone around them.

"Yeah? You think so?"

I smile at him, wide and bright. "You know you are."

"Doesn't hurt to hear it from you."

There goes my heart again. Does he know he's doing this to me? Pulling me in a hundred different directions?

It'd be so much easier if he was your typical college athlete and slept with anything on two legs.

"Maybe the best I've ever seen."

"Now I know you're lying." Troy's laugh is big and bright.

"Hey!" I punch him in the shoulder. He barely flinches while I shake my fingers out from the connection with his rock-solid muscle. "I don't like hockey, but I liked watching you play. You should know that counts for something."

"I guess it should."

"You'll have your pick of teams when the draft comes around. I can say I knew you when."

"Oh yeah? You'll be watching when I'm drafted?"

I shrug a shoulder. "Maybe. As long as you keep playing like you are."

"What better motivation does a guy need than that?" Troy hefts his bag higher up on his shoulder.

"I would think an NHL paycheck would be pretty good motivation for you."

"Nah." He waves me off. "It's not about the money for me. I love this game more than anything."

"I know you do."

It's why he's so dedicated to his studies. He wants something to fall back on after his career is over.

"Hey." Harper inserts herself into the conversation. "Marcus and I are going to head out. Grab a bite to eat."

"I'll see you at home?" I give Harper a quick hug.

"Don't do anything I wouldn't do," she whispers in my ear.

The two of them head out, leaving Troy and me alone.

"Listen, I know it's still early, but I was wondering if maybe you, uh, would like to, uh, go out tonight?"

"What do you have in mind?"

It gives me a minute to wrap my head around what he's asking.

A date. Troy is asking me out on a date.

A date I really want.

"I've got something up my sleeve. That okay with you, Angie?"

Angie.

The way he says my name is like hot cocoa on a cold winter day. It warms me from the inside out. It shouldn't be as much of a turn-on as it is.

Damn him.

The very last thing I need to have is a crush on Troy Hollins. Tutoring him is one thing. A full blown crush? I need to squash it before the feelings have time to settle. Because feelings will only lead to problems.

Big ones.

But my mouth doesn't get the message.

"A date. I'd like that."

Chapter Twelve

TROY

"You sure you don't want to come out with us, Gladiator?" Randy asks as we head into the house.

"Positive."

Randy has done nothing but pester me about why I'm not going out with the team tonight, and he follows me to my room to keep asking.

Because I spent all afternoon with them, I want to spend my night with Angie.

And I know exactly where I'm taking her. With the team's annual open skate to raise money for the booster club having been this afternoon, I have all night with Angie.

And I don't want to waste a minute of our time trying to decide on the perfect thing to do together.

"Whoever she is, make sure you impress her."

I flip Randy off before grabbing a new shirt to change into. "I know that. I'm not an idiot."

"Sometimes I question it."

"Why do I put up with you?" I laugh to myself as I slip into a new white, short-sleeved button-up shirt. It makes my biceps look good. Something I know Angie seems to like on me if her staring is anything to go by.

"You love me." Randy gives me a cheesy grin. "I'm assuming you won't be back here in time for the party tonight?"

"Do you ever get tired of partying?" I ask him.

"Never. Not when there's women to be had."

"Dude. That's sick."

I'm surprised the guy doesn't have an STI at this point.

"You're missing out."

"I'll take your word for it."

I'm glad I don't have to share a room with him. Really wish I had my own room, but it's some dumb hockey tradition—one of the dumber ones the team has. Instead of spreading out and actually having our own rooms, one of the teams back in the day decided the team all had to stay together in one house.

Over the years, we've grown into two houses to fit all the guys, but it still sucks. I want the privacy of my own room to bring someone home.

Not that I do it that often. I've never been one for puck bunnies. The younger guys love them. Not me. Not like Randy does.

Now that I've actually met someone, I want to be able to take her somewhere private.

Which, based on Randy's plans for the evening here, I won't get.

Spritzing on a spray of cologne, I'm out the door. "Stay out of my room tonight, Randy!"

"No promises!"

I ignore him as I head out to my Jeep to get Angie.

I'm nervous. More nervous than I should be for a first date. I don't take it lightly that Angie said yes to me. She could have very well told me to fuck right off and that's it. No more tutoring or anything.

But she said yes.

As I pull up to the curb outside of her building, I'm so fucking thankful she did.

Because holy shit.

Angela Brooks-Young is the sexiest woman I have ever laid eyes on. Tight dark jeans cling to her legs. The bright red sweater she's wearing hangs off one shoulder, showing off a black lace tank. Her hair is curling around her shoulders.

I'm about ready to say screw our plans and take her back upstairs to her apartment. Because I don't know how I'm expected to make it through the night without showing her everything I feel for her.

And I fucking want it all.

Parking the car, I hit the flashers and jump out.

"Hey, Angie." My voice is breathy as I approach her. I sound like a fucking high schooler who's out on his first date.

"Hey. You look good." Her eyes rake over me, and it takes everything in me not to flex my muscles to show off for her.

The hard part is over. I got her on a first date.

Now I'm only hoping for more.

"Not as good as you." I flip her hair behind her shoulder, resting my hand there.

"Aren't you a smooth talker?" Angie's mouth turns up into a small smile.

"Can I kiss you?" It's out of my mouth before I can stop myself. "Sorry, I didn't mean to ask that."

"You can."

"Wait, really?" I'm shocked by her answer.

Instead of telling me yes, she pushes up onto her toes and kisses me.

Her lips are soft and taste like vanilla. Wrapping an arm around her waist, I pull her in closer. I tease her bottom lip, dragging my tongue along it. Angie's hands fist into my shirt as I slide my tongue inside her sweet mouth.

I tilt her head to the side and deepen the kiss. Her tongue matches mine, stroke for stroke. I can't get enough. I chase her taste, wanting to discover everything she likes.

"Get a room!" someone yells out from a window above us.

"Sorry." I step back, adjusting my jeans and putting some distance between the two of us. It helps to cool the electricity buzzing through me.

A blush creeps up Angie's cheeks. "S'okay. I started it."

"Troublemaker." I wink at her before opening the door for her and helping her up. She doesn't need it, but any excuse to touch her.

"Where are you taking me?" Angie asks as I get in the car and point us in the direction we need to go.

"It's a surprise."

"Hmm."

"Good hmm?" I sneak a glance at her.

"I don't mind surprises, but I always like guessing where we're going."

"Okay." I reach across the console and rest a hand on her leg. "Hit me with your best guesses."

"Hockey game."

I pull up to a red light and look over at her. Face completely neutral. "I'm not that lame, Angie."

"I know. Movies?"

"Nope."

"Dinner?"

"There will be dinner," I confirm.

"Good thing I'm hungry then." Her much smaller hand closes over mine. Flipping it over, I link our fingers together.

"Are you now?" I squeeze her hand tighter. Her words drive me crazy. I'm hungry for more than just dinner. Hungry for everything she'll give me.

"I guess you'll have to find out just how much." She drags a finger up my arm.

Fuck. Me.

I am not going to make it through this date with Angie touching me like this. I've never craved anyone like this before. Angie has awakened something inside me that I never knew existed, which is insane, since I haven't even been with her yet.

"The zoo?" I get us here on autopilot, trying to push down every thought of Angie's naked body.

I nod. "They have a really good fall fest. Lots of good food and drinks."

"I don't think I've ever been."

Helping her out of the car, I link our hands again and we walk to the entrance.

"To the zoo?" I hand over our tickets and we go through the turnstiles.

Angie laughs. The setting sun reflects off her brown eyes, lighting them up. "I've been to the zoo. I used to cry when I was little."

Jesus. This might turn out to be the worst first date ever.

"You did?"

Angie nods, tucking a piece of hair behind her ear. "Yeah, but I got over it as I got older once I realized they were helping the animals. What I meant was I've never been to a festival here."

"My parents took us when we were younger. We'd get

our faces painted, eat churros, and get to stay up late. It was a special day."

"You and your sister, I'm assuming?" Angie asks.

I order two beers from a vendor near the elephant exhibit and pass one off to Angie.

"Yeah. She wanted to be an elephant for the longest time before she discovered how good she was at hockey."

Angie nearly spits out her beer. "She wanted to be an elephant? She knows that wasn't possible, right?"

"She does now. But try telling that to a sad little girl who wanted nothing more than to play with them and splash in the water."

Angie covers her mouth, laughter burbling out of her. "That might be the cutest thing ever. I'd like to meet your sister."

"Yeah?"

She nods. "Why do you sound so surprised?"

"I don't know. I figured you wouldn't want anything to do with my family."

I guide us under the trees to the stone wall that keeps the elephants in their exhibit. A chain link fence extends a good twelve feet into the air. Rocks and trees are spread out before us as one elephant drinks from the pond in the middle.

"Hey." Angie takes my chin in hand and turns my focus to hers. "I was wrong, before. About you."

"You were?"

"Yeah. I mean, I wouldn't be here if I wasn't. I made a snap judgment based on others and I'm sorry."

"I appreciate that." I drop an arm around her shoulders and pull her in close.

"I really like you, Troy."

"I really like you too, Angie." I press a kiss onto the top of her head, burying my smile there.

The elephant trumpets out, startling both of us.

"Jesus."

Angie bursts out laughing, beer spilling over the edge of her cup. "I think he was sad we weren't paying him any attention."

"I can't help it if all I want is you."

"So cheesy." Angie laughs and heads to the next exhibit.

Food vendors line the concrete sidewalks as we walk from habitat to habitat. As the night goes on, Angie gets more comfortable around me, mimicking animal poses as we go.

"Is that supposed to be a flamingo?" My gut hurts from laughing so hard. Angie is standing on one leg, the other bent out toward the side.

"Maybe if I was wearing all pink it'd look better."

"Angie, that is the worst impression of a flamingo I've ever seen."

She sets her foot down and crosses her arms over her chest. "Okay then, let's see you do it."

"I'll do it better than you."

I mimic her pose, but stick my arms out like chicken wings and stretch my neck as high as I can.

"Oh my God!" Angie starts laughing at me almost immediately. "That's even worse than me."

"I'm doing these birds more justice than you are."

None of them look that interested, skimming the water with their beaks to find food.

"I can't believe we're doing this." Angie presses her hands to my sides, breaking my position. "We look like idiots."

"I don't know. You'd make a pretty cute flamingo." I eye her up and down. "Although, you'd make a cuter penguin."

"You liked my waddle better?"

I slip my hands around her waist and slide them into the back pockets of her jeans. "I can't help it if your ass looked really good doing it."

A heated look washes over Angie's features. She bites down on her bottom lip. I want to pull it out, but my hands are quite content where they are. I drag her closer to me.

"You want to come back to my place?"

"Yes." The answer is out of me without thought. "God, yes."

How can one kiss from earlier still be driving me wild? If I don't experience everything with Angie tonight, I might explode.

"Then what are we waiting for?"

Chapter Thirteen

ANGIE

My nerves are at an all-time high as Troy follows me up the stairs to my second-floor apartment. Tension was thick on the drive home. Both of us want this. I want to spend the night with the man who has consumed my every waking thought.

We're both quiet as I unlock my door and link hands with him. His eyes don't stray from me. The apartment is quiet. No doubt Harper is out with Marcus right now.

"Nice room," Troy tells me as I shut the door behind him.

I did a quick clean before I left. Made the bed, stacked my books on my desk, but not much else. Clothes are neatly piled in the small closet, and pillows decorate my bed. The curtains are open to the courtyard out back. The desk lamp gives the room a soft glow.

"It's nice I don't have to share."

"You're telling me." A wolfish grin lights up his face.

"Do you want to keep admiring my room?" I sit down at the end of the bed and kick off my booties.

"Fuck no."

Troy pushes me back and hovers over me. The heat in his eyes has me squirming below him. Dark brown hair flops over his eyes.

It's dim in here, but I can see in his eyes exactly what he wants. The object of his desire.

Me.

I've never felt this wanton as Troy drags a finger down my chest and over my stomach.

"I've dreamed about this."

"Yeah?" My voice is breathy, cheeks heating at his words.

"This blush?" He drags his finger down my jaw. "I wonder if it's everywhere."

"Why don't you find out?"

I've never been this brazen, but Troy brings it out in me.

"I plan to." Troy pushes the bottom of my sweater up and drops a warm kiss on the soft skin of my stomach.

It's like every nerve is fighting to get there. To feel his lips on mine.

He pushes it up farther, fingers brushing against the lace bralette I'm wearing. My nipples are diamond hard at the slightest touch of him.

"I like seeing what I do to you." Troy nips at the hard peak below the fabric.

"Gah!" My hands slide down his back, pulling him into me. "So good."

My words are moans. I want more. Everything this man will give me.

"Lift up." Troy's hand pulls me up as he lifts my sweater up and over my head.

His eyes rake over me.

"I knew it." This time, his smile is cocky.

"Knew what?"

"You'd flush all over." Looking down, I see my chest is red.

"I can't help it if I want you."

Troy attacks my mouth with pure lust and desire. It's messy and wet and so damn good, I'm arching my hips up to meet his hard cock.

"You want more?" Troy pulls away, licking a path to my ear.

"Yes. I need to feel you."

Troy sits back on his knees and undoes each button of his shirt. One slow unfastening at a time.

I'm practically drooling by the time he opens it up and slips it off his shoulders. A light dusting of hair covers his chest. Abs for days meet the V of his hips as a happy trail leads to the band of his boxers sticking out above his jeans.

"It's unfair you look this good." Reaching out, I track the lines of his abs. I want to commit them to memory. I don't know what's going to happen with the two of us, but I want to make good use of the time we do have.

"I can say the same about you, Ang."

Troy hefts me into his arms and moves us up the bed.

I find his lips again and pull him in for another slow, long kiss. It's lust-inducing. The only thing that matters right now is his lips on mine. Hands explore our half-naked bodies as we taste and take.

I wiggle my hips to take more of Troy. His weight is delicious as it settles in the perfect spot. The way his cock settles against my pussy—even with layers of fabric between—hits just right.

"Too many clothes," I whine.

"So demanding." Troy nips at my ear before moving his hands up my body. This time, he pushes the lace of my bra up and over my head. "Fuck, Angie."

He palms his cock through his jeans as he takes me in.

Troy opens the button of his jeans and flicks down the zipper. When he takes his dick out, I have no doubt my face matches his.

Want. Need. Fire.

"See what you do to me?" He gives himself a long stroke. "You are so fucking sexy, Ang."

"You're not so bad yourself."

Sitting up, I wrap my hand around his own and feel the hard steel. Troy has the perfect boyfriend dick. Not too small, not too big. I cannot wait to feel it inside me.

He pulls his hand away as I play with him. Precum is leaking from the head. I run my thumb through it and rub it down him. Troy throws his head back in pleasure as I lazily jack him off.

"I could get off just like this," he moans.

"I'd like to see that."

Troy glances down at me. "While I'd love to cover you in my cum, that's not happening tonight."

"What's going to happen?"

Stepping off the bed, Troy grabs one of my legs and pulls me to the edge. He makes quick work of my jeans and underwear and then strips out of his own.

"What's going to happen is I'm going to eat this pretty little pussy of yours." Troy drops to his knees and pulls my ass to the edge of the bed. My legs are thrown wide over his shoulders.

"And then?"

"And then"—his mouth hovers over my clit—"you're going to come on my tongue. Before you even finish, I'm going to be sliding into you and making you come again on my cock before I come inside you."

Oh God. I want it all.

"Yes."

Troy's mouth kisses his way along my inner thigh. I

push up onto my elbows so I can watch him. His eyes are glued on mine as he moves to the other leg. Bastard is taking his time. I want that dirty mouth on me more than I want my next breath.

"Something you need, Ang?" He pulls back, quirking an eyebrow at me.

"You know I do."

"This?" He tugs one side of my pussy between his lips and I damn near explode.

"Yes!"

"Mmm, I don't know." The vibrations have me growing wetter and wetter. "Might need to test this side."

He mirrors the same thing on the other side. The way he's licking and sucking my folds has me dying. Every time I'm close to the edge, he stops and pulls back.

Troy is making me crazy. His lips are shiny with my need for him—a wild need that is taking hold in every cell of my being and threatening to explode.

"Please don't stop."

"Oh, I don't plan on it." This time, Troy doesn't tease. He sucks my clit into his mouth and gives it every bit of attention I'm demanding.

Licking.

Sucking.

Flicking.

Every pass of his tongue against that tight bundle of nerves pushes me that much closer to coming.

Troy is an expert. He moves his attention to my opening and slides his tongue inside. I'm pulsing with need.

"You taste amazing, do you know that?" Troy asks.

"No."

"You do. So sweet. So delicious. Like I knew you would be."

He blows a warm breath over me, and it tips me over the edge into the abyss.

"Troy!" I shout his name as everything inside me shatters.

Stars burst behind my eyes as his mouth drinks in everything I'm giving him. My hands fist in his hair as I hold him to me.

I've never felt more alive as my entire body—right down to my toes—lights up for him.

"Holy fuck, Angie. That was incredible."

I pull him down to kiss him. It's a heady sensation, tasting my own orgasm on his lips. I never thought I'd like that. But with Troy? I do.

I love that he brings out this side in me.

"Are you ready to fulfill step two of your promise?"

"You coming on my cock?"

"Yes."

"One orgasm and you're not ready to stop?"

"I don't know if I'll ever get enough orgasms from you," I confess.

"Then your wish is my command."

Troy bends over and fishes a condom out from his wallet. He opens the foil packet, but I sit up and grab it from him.

"Let me."

I don't put it on immediately. I'm eye level with him and want to taste him too. Giving him a wicked look, I suck the head of his cock into my mouth.

"This isn't what I had in mind for tonight." Troy makes no move to stop me though, only brushing my hair back from my face.

The salt hits my tongue, driving me forward. I can't take much before I'm pulling off him and sliding back down. I wrap my fist around the base and work him over, his hands on either side of my head.

Guiding me. Teaching me. Telling me exactly what he wants.

It's never been like this for me. It was a quick get in, get off, get out.

With Troy, we're doing this together. My pleasure was first for him. It's only fair that I show him the same in return.

Something I desperately want.

"Fuuuuck." Troy pulls me off him. "I'm too close, and I'm not coming in that pretty little mouth of yours tonight."

"You're not?" I wipe the spit that's gathered at the corner of my mouth with the back of my hand.

"No. I'm coming in that tight little pussy of yours."

I don't delay, pulling the condom out of the package and rolling it down his wet cock. I move back to the head of the bed, watching as he prowls toward me.

Troy wastes no time, lining himself up and pushing inside.

"Oh Troy…" He fills me full, but it feels incredible.

"Perfect. You feel perfect."

As Troy starts small thrusts, I pull him down for a kiss. There isn't an inch of space between us as every part of our bodies connects.

The brush of his chest against mine has my need amping back up. Each jack of his hips stretches me around him, letting me take more of him.

When he hits that spot inside me, I'm ready to come undone again.

"Fuck. I need you to come," Troy grits out. He hoists my leg up higher and moves faster. Goes deeper.

The change in angle does it. This orgasm isn't as strong as the first one, but no less exhilarating.

"Yes! Yes! Yes!" I chant, pulsing around him as I feel his release spill into the condom.

He comes on a groan. His head is thrown back and the veins in his neck pulse. Troy collapses on top of me. Both of us are breathing hard. I keep him close to me. The feel of him against me like this does something to my insides.

Whatever I was feeling for Troy before tonight has nothing on what I'm feeling for him now. This connection between the two of us is strong. One that I don't want to sever.

Can't bring myself to sever.

Troy slips out and scoops me into his arms as we lie together, bodies sticky with sweat. "Give me a minute and I'll clean us up."

"It's okay." I drag my fingers up and down his chest.

Because I want to stay with him like this as long as possible.

Troy is weaving himself into my life, and I don't know if I want to stop it.

Being with him is about as close to perfect as it can get, and I'll take every minute I can of this.

For as long as possible.

Chapter Fourteen

TROY

"Why do you look so nice?" Randy asks, looking up from the video game that he just died in.

"Going out."

"It's a Thursday." He shifts on the couch, letting the game reload. "You can't go out."

"Why not?"

"There's a party over at the football house. We always go. They have the best booze and women there."

"What's wrong with wanting to do something different?" I run a nervous hand through my hair.

Whatever this thing between Angie and me is, we're keeping it on the down low. As much as I'd like to tell everyone we're dating, I know we can't. Because she doesn't want it getting back to her dads.

Even though Marcus and Harper know, they're not going to tell anyone. And telling Randy who I'm going out with is completely out of the question. He'd blab about it to everyone.

"You don't want to get laid tonight?"

"Jesus. Is that all you care about?" I whack him on the

head as I walk into the kitchen to grab my keys from the small bowl we keep there. "We have an early practice tomorrow, so don't go fucking around tonight and be dead on the ice tomorrow."

"Please." Randy goes back to the game, one I haven't played with him in a while. "I can rebound with the best of them. You sure you don't want to be my wingman tonight? Party starts at ten."

Looking at my watch, it's only seven now. Even with what I have planned for Angie, I could be back in time to go to the party.

"Nah. I'm good. You have fun."

"Oh, I will." There's a cockiness to his tone that tells me it's all but a guarantee. I have no doubt that he'll have zero trouble landing anyone he wants tonight.

Perk of being an athlete on campus.

That'd never been for me. So many girls throw themselves at any one of the players on campus. My dad taught me better—to never take advantage of someone like that.

And I haven't.

Which is probably the only reason Angie gave me a chance. I know her history with players. That guy was a dick. I don't want to prove her right again.

"Stay out of trouble," I call to Randy, but he's not paying attention, yelling at the TV. A few of the guys are coming into the house from a late class, and I wave at them before getting into my Jeep to get Angie.

I'm more nervous than I should be as I head to pick her up. I didn't think we'd be here. After the other night, something changed between the two of us.

I felt it and I know she did too. Fuck, it was amazing.

Angela Brooks-Young has ruined me for every other woman, and that has come as a complete surprise to me. I never went to her with the intention of starting something. I really did go to her needing help with my classes.

Campus is busy tonight. Students are coming and going from the faculty buildings as the quad starts to fill up with early evening classes letting out.

With my hockey schedule, most of my classes are in the morning, leaving me with all the time for early practice before class and our afternoon skates.

I take the shortcut through the center of campus to Angie's place, and she's there waiting for me on the front steps.

Fuck, is she ever gorgeous. She's wearing a simple white dress, covered in what looks like red flowers, that's pulled over her knees. A jean jacket covers her shoulders to ward off the chill in the late fall air.

I could sit here for hours and never get tired of looking at her. I've always known about Angie—it was hard not to when her family grew up hating ours. I never thought our paths would cross.

Yet, here I am. Staring at the most beautiful woman I've ever seen. Thankful that she took a chance on me.

Hopping out of my car, I cover the distance between the two of us, wanting her in my arms. Her gaze lands on me, lighting her entire face up in a smile.

"Hey."

"Hi." I drop a kiss on her cheek and take a deep breath of that sweet, vanilla scent of hers. Damn, does it ever do things to me.

"You look great."

"You didn't really give me much to go on." She laughs.

"How does a rooftop movie sound tonight?"

"That sounds great."

It's not a far drive from campus. Being with Angie is

easy, talking the entire ride over. Parking in a garage nearby, I help Angie out and we walk over to the building.

"It's not going to be some hockey movie, is it?" Angie leans in closer.

"I thought I convinced you to like hockey already."

Angie looks up at me as we stop at the crosswalk, her brown eyes soft in the fading light. "I like watching you play. Jury is still out on everyone else."

I tuck a stray lock behind her ear. "I guess I can live with that."

"I really hope you level Kyle later this season."

I bark out a laugh as the light changes and we head in the direction of the theater. "I plan on leveling the shit out of him."

"I'll enjoy watching it."

"Look at you. You're just like the rest of us loving the hits of the game."

"Yeah yeah."

We reach the doors and head inside. It's a quick elevator ride up that spits us out into the lobby.

Heavy velvet lines the walls with gold sconces giving it ambient lighting. A well-stocked bar lines one wall with drinks and movie snacks.

I pay for the two tickets, a bucket of popcorn, and drinks. Night has settled as we walk out to the theater.

A white screen hangs on the opposite end. Double Adirondack chairs are arranged in rows on the Astroturf that lines the roof. String lights hang from the columns in the back. A basket of blankets sits by the door.

"Think we need one?" There's a slight chill to the air this time of year.

"Yes." Angie grabs one as I find an empty spot away from the crowd. She wastes no time snuggling in beside me.

"This is perfect." Angie takes a handful of popcorn and pops a piece in her mouth.

"I thought you'd like this."

"How did you know?" She turns to me, resting her chin on my shoulder.

"A romantic movie under the stars? I had a gut feeling."

Angie shifts and points toward the sky. "Quick, name that constellation."

I groan. "You think you're funny, don't you?"

The pleased smile on her face is answer enough for me. "I know I am."

"Whatever you say, Ang."

The hanging lights dim as the movie starts.

"I love this movie," Angie whispers to me.

I wrap an arm around her shoulders and pull her closer to me.

The Princess Bride plays in the background, but it's hard for me to focus on anything that isn't Angie. Every stray thought of mine is on the woman sitting next to me. I want more than just my thoughts on her, but with the way the seats are situated, we don't have much privacy.

Angie is lighting up every one of my senses. I've never been so aware of a person before. Of every soft sigh or giggle during a movie.

As the movie goes on, she nestles closer to me. I press a kiss to the top of her head. It's like we do this all the time. Something that is a part of our everyday life.

It's so easy being with her like this that it makes me think it's possible. I have no idea what our future holds. We have a big barrier to overcome if we plan on taking this thing further.

A cold drop on my face breaks me from the train of

135

thought. Shrieks ring out as the skies open up, a cold rain starting to pelt us.

"Oh my God!" Angie pulls the blanket from our laps over us. Her laughter is light as everyone scrambles for cover. "Was this all part of your plan tonight?"

"It definitely wasn't supposed to rain." Not that I checked the weather to know.

The blanket soaks quickly, doing little to keep us from getting wet.

"Think we should make a run for it?" Angie asks.

"Yeah."

Popcorn buckets and drinks are strewn across the fake grass. I grab the blanket and ball it up and set it on the chair. Angie darts toward the lobby, but I don't get that far.

Her dress sticks to her body, wet hair hanging down in waves around her.

"Why are you just standing there?" she asks, coat held half over her head.

"You know that's not doing you any good, right?" I point to the jacket in question. "You're already soaked."

She drops her arms and stands there. Face skyward, she takes my breath away. The movie stops and it's only the two of us out here now.

We've lost our minds, standing out here in the rain like this, but I don't care. Stalking toward Angie, I sweep her up into my arms.

"Shouldn't we get inside?" Her breath is warm against my cold lips.

"I don't care."

I capture her lips in mine, soaking in every ounce of pleasure I can from her. Her taste is buttery from the popcorn. It draws a smile from me as I deepen the kiss. I have no idea if anyone is watching us, but I don't care.

Angie wraps her arms around me. We give and take,

tongues tangling as the rain pours down around us. I couldn't have dreamed up a better night for the two of us.

"I can't believe it started raining." Her head is thrown back in laughter.

"There's no one else I'd rather kiss in the rain than you."

Angie spins, running inside. "You know, if you don't have a future in hockey, you could write rom-coms."

"I think I'll stick to hockey."

And hope that I get to have this woman by my side through whatever future I have.

Chapter Fifteen

TROY

ANGIE

We've got our astronomy final next week

TROY

THANK FUCK

Someone's ready to be done

With Professor Craig? Yeah

I'll miss having class with you

Tell me something I don't know

I can't stop thinking about you

Really?

Uh-huh

I haven't been able to stop thinking about you either

Even during hockey?

> Well, maybe not during hockey

I see where I fall in the line of things

> Who are you? Do I know you?

Ha ha. Very funny <<eye roll emoji>>

> Seriously, who are you?

Well, I guess it was nice knowing you

> Okay, now that's not funny

See? :P

> It's my charming personality, right?

So charming...so, study session today?

> I have practice

So after?

> I'll see you there

"Hollins. My office."

I groan at hearing the bark from Coach Morris.

"What's that about?" Marcus asks, setting the weight bar in its stand.

"No doubt about my grades."

"I thought you were doing better?"

"I am. Unless I fucked something up."

And with the semester ending next week, I won't have time to do anything about it.

"Relax. Maybe he's just calling you in to congratulate you."

"With that tone?"

"Stay positive." Marcus chucks his sweaty towel at my face.

"Gross, man."

"Just trying to distract you."

I flip him off as I head to Coach's office. Marcus and I came in early to get a workout in before our practice today. With finals and Christmas break coming up, I'm full of nervous energy.

I don't want to fuck up everything I've been working so hard for. SDU is currently at the top of the standings, and if we keep it up, we'll get an automatic bid to the playoffs.

Everything I've been working toward these last four years is about to come to a head. And I'll be damned if I fuck it up now.

"Everything okay, Coach?" I stand in the open doorway.

"Why would you think it wasn't?"

"No offense, but it's like getting called to the principal's office when you ask to see me."

He laughs, leaning back in his chair. "No need to bull-shit. I need to see you, I need to see you."

"So what's up?"

"I reached out to your professors to see how you're doing."

"And?" I swallow, trying to settle the nerves that are threatening to explode out of me.

"Whatever you're doing, I expect you to keep it up next semester. A B- in calculus and a B+ in astronomy. Excellent work, Troy."

"Seriously?" I know a few quizzes were still pending,

but I didn't realize I managed to pull my grades up that high.

"I know school isn't the easiest for you, but I'm proud of you."

"Thanks, Coach. This team means a lot to me and I'd hate to disappoint you."

"You're one of the finest young players I've had the privilege of coaching. I'm excited to see where the future takes you."

"I only hope that I've impressed the scouts this season."

"You have. I've heard good things from Colorado and Nashville. Maybe even Chicago."

"Wow."

Colorado would be the dream. Angie and I have talked about where I could end up. She wants to be in Denver, working for her dad's organization. I know she does, and I want that for her.

More than that, the Colorado Black Diamonds are among the elite teams in the league. Nashville? They are at the bottom. A bunch of dirty players if I've ever seen them. I want to play for a team with class. One that respects the game of hockey.

Chicago would also be good for me.

"Any team would be lucky to have you, Troy."

"I hope so."

I'd be happy with any team drafting me. There's still a lot of hockey left to play.

He nods his head. "Now go get out on the ice before I make you do backcheck drills."

"Yes, sir."

I hurry back to the empty locker room to change into my gear and get onto the ice. A wave of relief sweeps through me.

As long as I don't fuck up my finals too badly, I'll be able to keep my starting line on the team.

All because of Angie.

I don't think I would have made it through this semester without her. In fact, I know I wouldn't have. It's all thanks to her that I'm here.

It puts a dopey smile on my face as I skate through practice. This far into the season, I'm prone to aches and pains. But I ignore them all because I'm riding the high of everything this last year of school has brought me.

My starting place on the hockey team.

Grades I didn't expect.

Angie.

She was the biggest surprise of all.

Not even conditioning drills can take the smile off my face.

"Dude. Whatever you're thinking, stop it." Marcus is breathing hard next to me. It's our last set of drills before practice ends.

"I'm not thinking anything, Wizard."

"Oh yeah? You look like you just got laid."

"Knock it off." I shove at him. "Can't a guy be happy?"

"Not when we're getting our asses handed to us."

Coach blows the whistle and I take off skating toward the blue line. As soon as my skate hits it, I'm back in the other direction before turning and skating toward center ice.

I hate these drills. The worst of the worst.

Today I'm able to push through because I know what's waiting for me.

There's a pep to my step as I leave the rink and head to meet Angie. I could get used to this.

I really could.

I take the well-worn path to the study rooms that Angie

always books for us. I like that she wants us to have a private space to study. No point in sitting out in the middle of the library where everyone can come up and interrupt us.

"Hey Ang."

"Someone's in a good mood."

I drop down into the seat next to her and give her a loud smacking kiss on the cheek. "My coach told me that my professors emailed him that my grades are passing. Well, good actually."

"Are you serious?"

Her excitement matches my own.

"He said to keep it up next semester."

"So I guess what you could say is that I'm keeping my starting position too?" She waggles her eyebrows at me.

"You, Ms. Brooks-Young, are not going anywhere."

Not for a very long time, if I have any say about it.

Chapter Sixteen

ANGIE

I've got something planned for us this afternoon

Oh yeah? <<sly face emoji>>

Troy!

Can't blame a guy for trying

See if I take you anywhere

I promise I'll be good

When does hockey practice get out?

Three

I'll pick you up

And maybe if I'm good…

Troy!

. . .

"This is your favorite road trip snack?" Troy asks, popping the bag of corn chips. "It's so…"

"So what?" I ask, reaching in and grabbing a cheesy chip.

"Basic." His brown eyes are playful.

"Consider me basic, then, Troy."

Troy grabs my wrist, pulling me close. "You, Angie, are anything but basic."

He sucks my finger between his lips.

His eyes darken with lust as they study me. His tongue swirls around the pad of my finger, sending desire straight to my core.

It has me wanting to throw our plans to the wind.

"You're a distraction." My voice is breathy as Troy pulls my finger out of his mouth.

He leans over and gives me a quick kiss. "Not as much as you."

"If we don't leave now, we won't get there in time."

It's midafternoon. With Troy's practice today, we couldn't leave any earlier.

"Your fault."

"Mine?" I'm indignant. "Not a chance."

"Then let's get moving, Brooks-Young."

"If only I didn't have to wait on you to start this road trip."

"Does it count as a road trip if we're only driving to LA?" Troy asks, clicking the music over to a rock station.

"I can always drop you back off at your house if you don't want to go…" I give him the side eye as I merge onto the I-5.

"And miss spending the afternoon with you? Hell no."

It shouldn't give me so much satisfaction, but it does.

"Good. Because this will also be a good learning experience."

"Oh yeah?"

"If I have anything to say about it, yes."

Which I will.

Because when I planned today around Troy's practice schedule, I wanted it to work for both of us.

Me getting to spend the day with him and him learning something for astronomy.

For a late Saturday afternoon, the drive is easy. Without much traffic, we make it in good time, chatting about everything and nothing. If there's a silence, it's easy. Everything is with Troy. Not like with any other guy I've dated.

With the end of the semester fast approaching, I'm trying to squeeze in every minute I can with him. His practice schedule doesn't make it easy.

I don't know what's going to happen come spring. It has a ball of worry in my belly every time I think about it.

Griffith Observatory comes into sight as I guide us into the parking lot nearby.

"What are we doing here?" Troy asks as he steps out of the car. He's casual today, in gray sweats and an SDU long-sleeved hockey shirt. The backward cap on his head hides his unruly hair. I didn't really give him much time after practice.

"A good way to spend the evening together. Me with you and you learning something for astronomy."

Shrugging a shoulder, I walk up the path that leads to the white, stucco building. Troy doesn't let me get far, grabbing the sides of his hockey zip-up that I'm wearing.

"Ugh, can't a guy get a break?" he moans.

"Ouch. And here I thought this was a good idea."

I stalk up the path, ignoring the groups of people leaving the observatory. It shouldn't sting as much as it does that he wants a break from me. All I wanted was to spend time with Troy.

Was that really too much to ask?

"Easy there, tiger." Troy grabs my hand and pulls me off the sidewalk and onto a bench. "I didn't mean a break from you."

Warm lips press a kiss onto my neck. Heat courses through me from the smallest contact. "You didn't?"

"Never." His breath ghosts over my neck. "Why would I ever want a break from you, Angie?"

Troy's hand rubs a comforting path along my thigh. "God, I sound so insecure."

"I only meant a break from studying." His eyes are dark pools of sincerity. "My brain is tired from memorizing all the equations."

Cupping his face in my hands, I rub my thumbs over the apples of his cheeks, tracing the faint scar he got playing hockey in middle school. "I promise, there will be no equations today."

"You promise?" He gives me the smile I love so much.

I nod. "I promise, Troy. Just you and me enjoying the stars."

"Then how about we get going then?"

I steal a quick kiss from him before running up the sidewalk. His laugh hits my ears as he jogs up behind me.

"Now you're trying to get away from me?" I'm pulled back against him.

"Never." I hand over our tickets and wait for them to be scanned before heading inside.

"You know,"—Troy looks around the lobby of the observatory—"in all the years I've lived in SoCal, I've never been here."

"Really?" I link our hands together and walk toward the first exhibit.

"Hockey was always my biggest priority." He shakes his head. "Maybe if I spent more time studying, I wouldn't be as worried about my grades."

"But then we wouldn't have met," I tell him.

"Do you really think so?"

"I don't know. You wouldn't have come to the tutoring center that day, and I wouldn't have told you no. And then why would you have any reason to help me at your party?"

"I still would have helped you, Angie."

"It's because you're a good person."

That's definitely something I've learned about him. Otherwise, I wouldn't be here with him right now.

Troy pulls me in close, my back to his front as we take in the exhibit around us. Maps of constellations line the walls. A telescope takes up the entire room, pointing toward space. Families are packed around us.

"This is what I thought astronomy would be like."

"Looking at the stars?"

"Yeah. All the equations and light years are over my head. I like looking at them."

"It's why I signed up to take the class."

"Not to show off what a smarty-pants you are?"

I elbow him in the side. "When have I ever showed off like that?"

"Never," he whispers by my ear. "Do we get to look at more stars?"

"C'mon." I grab his hand and walk toward the line wrapping around the telescope. It's one of the biggest draws of the observatory.

It doesn't take long for our turn to step up and see what everyone has been oohing and ahhing over.

"Okay, this is cool." Troy's face is lit up as he looks through the tiny hole. "You have to see this."

I take his place as he moves me in front of him. Stars

blanket the inky night sky. Some are brighter than others. Planets in blues and reds shine.

"It's beautiful."

"Can I see again?" Troy asks.

I step aside to let him look. Everything about him is fixed on this tiny blip of space. Whereas my entire world right now is focused on him.

"It's hard to focus."

"Why?" I ask him.

He steps back, taking my hand and pulling me close. "Because you're better than all the stars in the universe."

Troy's words have my breath catching in my throat.

It's a moment.

Brief.

Fast.

The line of people presses upon us to keep moving. But even these few seconds, seeing the stars with Troy, are ones I never want to lose.

I only want these moments with Troy.

No one else.

The clarity I'm hit with is like a freight train. I've never felt anything like it before.

Troy and I have only been together for a few months. I never expected anything like him coming into my life. I had big plans after college. I wanted to travel and see the world before starting to work at my dad's foundation.

That entire plan is about to be thrown out the window. Not that I still won't do it. But I want to do it with Troy. Fit him into my life.

That scares me.

Troy squeezes my hand and pulls me outside of the building. Night has fallen around us.

"You okay?"

Troy wraps me in his arms as we take in the lights of the city spread out before us.

"Yeah, I'm good."

"Good."

We stand there, watching LA come to life before our eyes. If only I can make that *good* permanent.

Because I want Troy. And I'll be damned if I lose him.

Chapter Seventeen

ANGIE

"I can't believe I let you talk me into this."

"Think of how cute you're going to look skating."

"Maybe to you," I grumble.

"Admit it. You think I'm hot when I'm playing hockey." Troy's smile lights up his entire face as he laces up the last of my skates.

"I will do no such thing." I fight the laugh that threatens to burst free.

"Yup, totally sexy when I'm playing." Troy taps my foot. "Now I get to see you out on the ice."

"I'm going to be terrible."

Troy and I are the only two people here. It's late. Later than the rink is usually open. I guess it's one of the perks of being on the hockey team.

"I'll make sure you don't fall."

Troy pops up on his skates with ease and grabs my hands. I'm like a baby horse learning to walk. Hobbling my way over to the open gate, Troy steps back onto the ice with me in tow.

"Holy shit!"

If Troy wasn't holding on to me, no doubt I would be flailing my arms and on the ice in under two seconds.

"Keep your balance centered. If you lean back, you'll fall."

"How do I know if I'm doing that?"

Troy skates closer to me, pulling me into a standing position. He moves my hands to his shoulders. "Hold on here. This will help."

"How am I supposed to move my feet?"

At this point, Troy is just pulling me across the ice. My own feet are doing nothing.

"Push off with the back and glide into it."

"Oh, that's it?" I laugh, looking down at my feet.

"Look at me. Looking down makes it harder to see where you're going."

"As opposed to looking at you?"

Troy's smile is easy, and it's one that I'm learning to love. "I should make it easy for you not to focus on your feet then."

"Fine."

I lock eyes with Troy. I try to ignore how warm his hands feel on my hips as they carry us over the ice. I'm hardly doing anything as we glide over the glassy surface.

"Is it getting easier?" Troy leans in closer, his lips ghosting over mine.

"No."

"It's not?"

I shake my head. "How am I supposed to concentrate on what my legs are doing when I'm focused on you?"

"I am pretty distracting."

"You wouldn't make a good teacher." I laugh.

"Then it's a good thing I don't plan on going into the profession."

"Or I should put a paper bag over your head so I can try to learn."

Troy laughs, echoing around the empty rink. "Then I guess I shouldn't tell you to picture me naked to make it easier?"

"You do not do that during tutoring sessions, do you?"

"I'd get nothing done if I did." Troy pulls back from me and I keep following him. "But I got you to skate on your own."

"You did?" I look down at my feet before glancing back up at Troy. "Holy shit! I'm doing it!"

"Looks like the student has become the master."

"I'll be coming for your starting spot any day now."

"You'd look good in a jersey, Ang."

I push off on my skates like Troy taught me and try to get closer to him. "Brooks-Young might not fit on a jersey. I think I'll stick to cheering you on."

"My favorite fan." Troy spins around me, which catches me off guard.

"Troy!"

I try to correct, but my feet come out from under me and I fall back into Troy, knocking us both down onto the ice.

He hisses. "It's a lot softer of a landing with gear on."

"I told you I wasn't good at this."

"You were getting the hang of it."

Troy shifts me off him, the ice cold under my jeans. Now that we're not skating, the boots are tight on my ankles.

"I couldn't do this every day."

Troy looks around him. "It's weird. That future involves a pair of skates and ice."

"Don't forget the stick."

"You're learning."

"I'm also learning that it's really cold being on the ice."

"C'mon then." Troy hops up with ease and pulls me to my feet. Instead of being shaky like I was the first time, I have a bit more confidence. We do a few more laps before heading back to the bench.

With my hands in his, I'd follow him just about anywhere.

A thought that is thrilling me more and more.

This thing with Troy is turning into so much more than just a tutor and her tutoree. It wasn't even a casual fling.

It's intense, these feelings I'm having for him. Like we bypassed the easy college relationship thing and it became so much more.

When he looks at me like that though? Like he is now? There's nothing better than that. No better feeling in the world than being his sole focus. Not even hockey can come between the two of us.

"If you get too good at this, Angie, I won't be able to teach you anymore."

I steal a kiss from him as we step onto the padded surface behind the boards. "Then maybe I'll keep being bad at it."

"Oh yeah?" A cocky grin spreads across Troy's face. "I think there's better ways to spend time with me than pretending to be bad at skating."

"Like…studying calculus?"

He shudders. "God no. I'm glad my final is in a few days and I can finally be done."

"Even done with me?"

I hate that I'm done with my classes early and am flying home so soon.

Troy sweeps me into his arms and plants a kiss on my lips. One that I feel in my toes. "I'm not done with you,

Angie. If I have my way, I won't be done with you for a very long time."

What few lights are left shut off. Only emergency lights remain. Troy and I are in our own little world here. A bubble I want to stay in.

I'm not ready to leave him. Not ready to head back home for Christmas break and face the real world. Face my dads for the first time since we started this thing.

"When do you get home from break?" Troy asks.

"I'll be home two days before school starts."

"Is it cheesy to say I'll miss you?"

"No." Because it has a feeling I don't want to give a name to blooming in my chest. "I'll miss you too."

More than I'm going to admit to him.

"I have something for you." Troy steps back, digging something out of his coat pocket. We're both still sitting on the bench, neither of us ready to leave.

"You didn't have to get me anything."

"Open it," Troy goads me.

It's a small box wrapped in red paper. The edges aren't done well, I'm guessing a sign that he did this himself. Which makes me appreciate it that much more. Cutting through the paper, I pop open the small brown box.

"Oh Troy."

It's a simple gold necklace with two intertwined stars. That's it. No diamonds or pearls.

"It's nothing big—"

I cover his mouth with my hand. "I love it."

I pull it out of the box and let it fall against my gloved hand. It's beautiful in its simplicity. The perfect representation of our relationship.

"You do?" His voice is quiet.

I don't have any words for how much this means to me,

so I pull him to me, showing him just how much I love it by sealing my mouth over his.

We get lost in each other. Every one of my senses is on fire.

The coolness of the rink.

The darkness surrounding us.

The scruff of Troy's mouth as it moves over mine.

The sweet taste of him as our tongues collide.

I could stay here all night. Wake up next to him and be perfectly content.

"I have an early morning flight to catch."

"I'll see you when you get back." Troy drags his nose along my jaw before pressing a kiss to my neck. "You'll call me while you're gone?"

"Every day."

Leaving Troy is harder than it should be. Christmas break is usually my favorite break. A few weeks at home with no school and being surrounded by family. I love it.

Now?

I'm already counting the days.

Chapter Eighteen

ANGIE

I miss the library

Who are you and what have you done with Troy Hollins

<<insert how rude gif here>>

The library? Really?

I'd rather be studying there with you

I thought you were having a good Christmas?

I am

So why do you want to be at the library?

My cousins are here

And?

And their kids are here too. I love my cousins' kids, but they are a lot of work

Aww...I can only imagine you as...can I call you Uncle Troy?

I'd rock being Uncle Troy, but I'm TIRED

Can't you wear them out playing hockey or something?

My cousin won't let them play until they're older

Why not?

Something about not being safe. I dunno

It's safer than football

I don't think that's a selling point

I can imagine you skating around with them

I've taken them skating. They're good

Uh-oh! Are they going to be better than you some day?

Maybe once I'm in the Hall of Fame, they'll carry on the family name

Getting pretty cocky there, aren't you?

Aren't you the one telling me it's not cocky if it's true?

Now you're listening to me?

I've been listening to you all semester. It's how I got a B- on my last astronomy test

> a B-? You didn't tell me that!

It didn't feel that important

> Of course it is! That's awesome, Troy! I'm so proud of you

All because of you ;)

> You're the one who did the hard work

"**A**ng! Movie time!"

"Coming!" I call down to my dad. It's our family tradition. After Christmas dinner, we always settle in for a movie. It started by the time Nick was born, and now it's a way for all of us to spend time together during the holidays.

Not that Nick or I are going anywhere. Because the one other person I want to spend time with over the holiday? I can't.

ANGIE

> Gotta go...Christmas movie with the fam

TROY

Anything good?

> Not sure yet...it's my brother's year to pick the movie

Good luck...talk later?

> Yeah <3

I BOUND DOWN THE STAIRS. My dads still live in the same house as when I was born. I love how cozy it is. Pictures of them together and with Nick and me line the walls. We've always been close. It's one of the things I love about our family.

"Want a glass of wine?" Dad holds the bottle of red out to me as I come in the room. No doubt it's a Malbec, his new favorite. One that I made sure to buy him this year.

"Sure." He's waiting in the kitchen that opens directly to the living room and dining room. I grab a glass from the bar that splits the kitchen and dining room and hold it out for him. The lights are already low for our movie.

"Can I have some?" Nick asks from his spot on the couch.

"Are you twenty-one and I didn't realize it?" Dad asks, setting the bottle down as I follow him into the living room. Cookies and snacks sit on the coffee table. Unwrapped presents are stacked under the Christmas tree in neat piles. Pictures from years of sitting on Santa's lap line the mantel.

"No. But I'm eighteen now," Nick whines. "I'll be going to college soon. Shouldn't I know the perils of drinking before then?"

"I don't see you going off to college and becoming a binge drinker," Pops tells him, dropping onto the couch next to Dad. The gray, cozy sectional takes up most of the living room. It faces the TV that hangs over the stone fireplace.

"He'll be just like Angela."

"You say that like it's a bad thing, Dad."

"Ang is a Goody Two-shoes," Nick says. "All she does is study."

"So do you!" I defend. "What's wrong with that?"

"Have you ever done anything that you're not supposed to?" He looks at me over his shoulder. "Saint Angela always doing whatever is asked of her."

"Nick!" Both my dads snap at him.

"Leave your sister be," Pops tells him. "Turn on the movie, okay?"

"Fine," he grumbles.

"Don't listen to your brother," Dad whispers to me as the movie starts.

"I usually don't." I laugh it off, but his words sting.

Is that how he sees me? Someone who will never step a foot out of bounds? Who only does what is asked of her?

If only he knew.

I'd hate to think that he'd be proud of me because of breaking all the rules. Neither one of us have ever been the rebels. It's just not in our nature.

Leave it to me to push back against everything I'm told not to do when I'm a senior in college. It's not like my dads are that strict.

Except I don't think they'd see it that way when it comes to Troy. They would lose their shit if they knew I was dating him.

God. If only there was a way out of this.

A way to keep Troy and my family happy.

I didn't think I'd have to worry about big life decisions like this until after college. I've known exactly what I've wanted to do since my dad started Team Rainbow. I've wanted to work for my dad for as long as I can remember.

He started the organization after he retired to help teams at all levels, from youth sports all the way to the professionals, to foster inclusivity in sports for LGBTQIA+ athletes. It's something he is passionate about, and I want to help further the organization after college.

I haven't had to worry about job interviews during

college or stress about where I wanted to live. It was always here in Denver.

Now? Now everything feels murky.

Troy. My job. Where the two of us stand post college. Our families.

"You okay, Ang?" Dad asks from beside me. It's gotten dark. The movie flashes across the open living room.

"I'm fine. Why?"

"You're quiet, is all."

"Thinking about school."

"Are you worried? I thought everything went well this semester."

"It did."

"All As," Pops interjects. "What's there to worry about?"

"It's my last semester. It feels weird that school is ending."

"I couldn't wait to be done with college," Pops says.

"Really? I thought you loved it?" I ask.

"I did. But I was ready to get out into the real world. I wanted to teach and start changing lives."

"You have done that." Dad drops a kiss on his forehead.

It makes my heart ache seeing the two of them together.

I want what they have. I always have. A love that supports and grows as we get old together. That no matter what comes our way, we face it together.

Is it too soon to hope that's what I have with Troy?

Can I even have it with him?

Nick lets out a snore from his spot on the couch. His book is flat across his stomach now.

"Alright. Maybe we should cut the movie short tonight."

"You sure?" I take another long sip of my wine. It helps to calm the swirling thoughts in my brain.

"Go, call your friends. Do things that college kids do."

"So go to bed early after getting up at the crack of dawn to open presents this morning?"

More like go back to texting Troy, but I'm not going to tell them that.

"Don't forget we're having breakfast tomorrow with Uncle Colin and Aunt Peyton."

"I won't." More people that won't approve of my relationship. "Love you guys."

"Love you, sweetheart."

I retreat back to the safety of my room and flop down onto my bed. Maybe tomorrow I'll have a clearer head. One that I can use to come up with a plan to try and figure this thing out with Troy.

It'd be a Christmas miracle if I could.

Chapter Nineteen

TROY

"You promised to feed me."

I ignore Angie, needing to feel her. The minute the door shuts to her room, I'm on her. It's been too damn long without my hands on her bare skin. Without the feel of her under me.

"After."

Two weeks was too long. The hunger I have for her is unlike anything else. My body craves her and everything she'll give me.

I never thought I could feel like this with someone. But Angie brings out feelings in me I never knew I could have.

My lips trail a hot path down her neck. The V-neck T-shirt she's wearing clings to her every curve.

"Troy…" Angie's voice is a moan as she walks us backward to her bed.

"God, I've missed you."

"Me too." She hooks a finger behind my belt and pulls me closer to her. "I'm so glad I came back early."

Grasping her chin, I turn her eyes to mine. "Did your dads give you a hard time?"

She shakes her head. "No. And I don't want to talk about them right now."

A wicked smile curls the corner of my mouth. "How about no talking then?"

"How will I tell you what I want?"

Grabbing the back of my shirt, I pull it up and over my head. Angie's eyes widen with lust as they rake over my bare chest. Those eyes of hers always give her away.

Her whole body, really.

Because with one move, I know exactly what she needs. I'm a quick study, learning everything she likes and dislikes and knowing exactly how to amp up her pleasure to new heights.

Making Angie come might be one of my favorite things in the world.

"I have a feeling I'll be okay."

Angie leans back onto her bed, situating herself in the middle. It's already dark outside. The overhead light in her room doesn't do much for us.

Doesn't bother me in the least. I know Angie's body like the back of my hand. Could map every detail, every nip and curve, with my eyes closed.

Closing the distance between the two of us, I settle my weight over her and reclaim her mouth.

Her lips are pliable under mine. Angie is just as eager as I am for this if her kiss has anything to say about it. We're both grappling for control. Warm, soft hands trail over my skin, sending zings to my cock.

She wants to get in on the action, but I have to wait. I want to take my time with Angie. Her kisses are intoxicating. I can't get enough. I could lie here and make out with her all night and it'd be enough.

Except for tonight. Tonight, I need every part of her she'll give me.

Pushing up onto my knees, I settle between her open legs. Her kiss-swollen lips are pouting up at me.

"Why'd you stop?"

"Because you have on far too many clothes for my liking, Ang."

Angie sits up and pulls her own shirt over her head, dropping it onto the floor next to her bed. Deft fingers unfasten her bra and it follows the same path.

Her dark nipples are already hard. I love seeing what I do to this woman. I drag a single fingertip over one hard peak before twisting it between my fingers.

"Are you already wet for me too?" I whisper.

"Why don't you find out?"

"Such a tease." I smile down at her before laying her back on the bed. Those gorgeous tits of hers will have to wait.

I make quick work of her jeans. There's a wet spot on the cotton of her underwear that I drag a finger through.

"I love that I make you like this."

"How do you make me?"

"Needy." Angie is squirming under me. Her skin is flushed. I pull her leg up onto my shoulder and press soft kisses to the inside of her knee. "I love knowing how much you need me."

"So much, Troy. I need you."

"Why do you need me?" I ask her, doing the same thing to her other leg. My hands drift up and down on the soft flesh of her thighs.

"To make me feel desired. And sexy."

I nip at the inside of her leg. "You don't need me to make you feel sexy. You do that all on your own."

Pushing my hands down farther, I brush my knuckle along her underwear.

"But no one has made me feel like this before. Only you, Troy. It's only you."

I can't wait another minute. Grabbing the flimsy material of her thong, I rip it from her body. I bury my nose in the sweet scent of it.

"So fucking good, Ang."

Dropping her legs to the bed, I bury my face between them. My fingers slide between her folds easily.

"God, you're perfect." I swipe my tongue through the wetness, swirling it around her clit. Her legs squeeze my head.

"More." Her voice is breathy as it escapes her.

"More what?"

"Everything. I want your mouth."

"Only my mouth?"

"To start with."

I smile against her pussy. "Aren't we greedy?"

Angie pops up on her elbows, looking down at me. Her hair is a disheveled mess. "You turn me into a crazy person whenever you're near me. I can't help it if I want you this badly."

"Not as much as I want you." I attack her pussy with a newfound hunger.

Licking. Sucking. Drinking up every last drop of sweet wetness that she's giving me.

"Troy!" Angie pushes her hands through my hair. The tinge of pain amps up my own need coursing through me. "Please don't stop."

"Please will get you everywhere."

Pushing her legs open wider, I drag my tongue up and down, swirling it in ways I know she loves. I drag her wetness down farther, knowing that a little ass play will always get her going.

Her pussy is squeezing my fingers as I curl them inside

of her. She's close to coming. She's grinding down on my face. Her juices are coating my chin.

"Are you going to come for me like a good girl?"

"Yes. Oh yes!" she shouts, finally coming around my fingers. I pull them out and lick up every drop of her release. It seems endless.

An arm is thrown over her eyes. Her entire body is sated. My cock is tenting in my pants. Seeing her like this sends a fire blazing through my veins.

The perfect fucking woman for me. The one that I love more than anything. And even if she might not be there yet, I'm going to spend the night showing her just how much she means to me.

Standing up, I push my own pants and boxers off and grab a condom from my wallet.

"Are you going to be up for more?" I lean over the bed, moving her arm off her face.

"I'll always want more with you, Troy."

"Good answer." I take her mouth in a searing kiss. She's tasting her own release on my lips.

It's so fucking hot when she's like this. I cover her tit with my palm and give it attention as she's kissing me. Her own hand wraps around my dick as we kiss.

I tear my lips from hers and drop my forehead to meet her own. "Shit, Ang. I don't want to come in your hand."

"It'd be hot."

I try to push her hand off me, but she holds on tighter.

My hips press forward, fucking the tight hold she has on me. It shouldn't be this hot. I can't remember the last time a hand job got me off.

But watching Angie as she gets me there is the sexiest thing in the world.

"If I'm coming like this, you're coming again."

I move my hand down her body to play with her pussy

again. I slide one finger inside her again with ease. She's still pulsing from earlier.

"I'll only come if you do." Fire is in her eyes as she fixes her gaze on me.

"Fuck."

My eyes are locked onto her hand, watching as she jacks me off. The way she twists her fingers over my cockhead drives me wild. She smears precum down my shaft, quickening her pace.

I pump my hips faster to match the pace of my own fingers working inside her again.

"Shit. I'm going to come."

As the first ropes of cum hit her chin, she leans up and sucks the head of my dick into her mouth.

"Oh fuck." I wrap my free hand into her hair and press farther inside her warm mouth. Her tongue swirls around the head as she captures each drop of my release.

Angie's pussy is squeezing my fingers as her moan vibrates around me. I love that getting me off gets her off.

Again.

Angie drags a single finger along the bottom of my dick as she pulls off, giving the head one last kiss before settling back onto her bed.

I head to the bathroom to clean up and get a warm washcloth to do the same for her.

"Fuck, Angie." I have no words for the woman lying spread out on the bed before me. Her naked body is a dream. I take my time, showing care for every last inch of her body before snuggling into her side.

My fingers drift over the soft curves of her skin. Angie rests her head on my bicep, giving me a happy smile. She fits perfectly beside me.

I lean down and kiss her. Our fingers and legs tangle as we kiss like our lives depend on it.

There's not a single worry in my head right now.

Angie. Angie is consuming every waking thought of mine. I never want to lose this with her.

Sure, the sex is some of the best I've ever had, but this? The quiet moments after? I want to wrap her in my arms and savor this feeling forever.

Now if only I can figure out how to get Angie on board.

Because there's no forever without her.

Chapter Twenty

ANGIE

There's a happiness floating through me that I haven't felt before. When I left for school this summer, I was sad. As much as I love school, I was ready to get my future started.

Now? I couldn't wait to get back from break. To get back to Troy. With a week before school starts, and him having optional hockey practice, I want to soak up every free minute we can have together.

Lying in bed together is heaven. With Harper still gone, the apartment is quiet. Until a loud rumble erupts from me.

"Oh my God," I say at the same time Troy says, "What was that?"

I cover my face with my hands.

"Was that your stomach?" Troy peels one hand off my face, a joyful smile greeting me.

"I said you needed to feed me!" The rumble sounds again, only this time louder.

"C'mon." Troy pops up and it takes me a minute to

focus on what he's doing. It's unfair that he is that sexy naked.

Hard, muscular planes. Toned ass. Biceps that I can easily make a pillow of.

Troy cuts off my perusal by tossing his T-shirt at my head.

"I thought you were hungry?"

"Can't I admire the sights for a minute?"

He fishes out his boxers and steps into them. "You can admire later. I don't need you passing out on me before round two."

"Ugh. Fine." I pull his T-shirt over my head and follow him out into the kitchen.

"Do you have anything to eat?"

I duck under him and open the freezer. "One bag of pizza rolls and a carton of strawberry ice cream."

"There's some chips and chocolate in here." Troy takes the bags out of the cabinet next to the fridge. "I guess this is going to have to tide us over."

"I don't think any of this meets your dietary require-ments for the team." I step over to the oven to preheat it for the pizza rolls and grab two spoons for the ice cream.

Troy shrugs a shoulder. "I had a good workout today. It should be okay."

Digging in to the ice cream, I take a mouthful. I sit on the island, watching as Troy spreads everything out and gets the pizza rolls ready for cooking. "I might be able to give you another workout tonight if you really need it."

Troy steps between my legs, grabbing the spoon and finishing my bite. "You don't have to ask me twice."

"Hey! Only if I am properly fed."

"Is this what life with you is going to be like?" Troy pops everything into the oven and grabs the chips to start eating. "Constantly making sure you're fed?"

What life with you is going to be like.

I know the meaning behind his words. He's planning a future. Just like I want to be.

But *how?*

I keep coming back to that thought. If I want this thing between the two of us to continue, I'm going to have to figure out a way to tell my dads.

Troy drops a kiss on my cheek and plates everything up before heading back to my room. "I'll order Thai just in case."

"My hero." I bat my eyelashes at him before grabbing two water bottles and trailing after him.

We snack and talk, catching up on what happened over break. The two of us talked every day while we were apart, but I still missed this. Being with him and talking and laughing. Nothing can ever replace what it's like to be with Troy in person.

Being surrounded by him is overwhelming in the best way.

I sigh happily, leaning into his side. "You know, next time, feed me and then sex." I pop a gooey pizza roll into my mouth.

He presses a kiss to the crown of my head. "Noted. I will starve myself of sex if it keeps you happy."

"I'm not asking you to do that." I laugh. "But maybe next time we can get food on the way home from the airport."

"Then don't be so damn irresistible that I have to get you home immediately."

"If this is what away games will be like, I need to prepare."

Troy spins, stretching out across me on the bed with his head in my lap. "You being hungry, or me having to bring you food?"

I run my fingers through his thick, silky hair and rest the other hand on his abs. "More so being ready for whenever you come home."

"If it means I'm coming home to you, I'm happy."

I don't know how we drifted into talk of the future. It makes me nervous, planning this way.

But I want to.

I want to make plans with Troy.

I only hope we get the chance to have those plans come to life.

Chapter Twenty-One

ANGIE

TROY

I'm glad it's a home game tonight

ANGIE

I've missed going to your games. Away games suck

I miss not seeing you in the stands…like the hockey fan I turned you into

I'm a fan of yours

Nah, admit it. You like hockey

Ugh, fine! I like hockey

My life's work is complete

Yeah, yeah

Will you be okay at the game? I know Harper isn't going

I'll be fine

> You sure? I know dickmeister will be there

> > Will you level him for me?

> As long as I don't get kicked out of
> the game

> > Don't do that, but you will get lucky

> Hit douchebag as hard as possible without
> getting kicked out...on it

> > My hero! <<heart eye emoji>>

> Anything for my girl

I'm nervous. I can't remember the last time I've been *this* nervous. All because Troy invited me to his game.

Not just any game. The game against Boston.

And my fucker of an ex.

That look on his face when he asked? The curl of his lips? The way he batted his eyes at me?

I couldn't say no.

When it comes to Troy, I find it hard to say anything but yes.

Pulling my red and black SDU hoodie over my head, I take a final deep breath before leaving my room. If I'm lucky, Harper will be gone tonight. I'm sure there's a study group somewhere that she needs to go to.

"Where are you off to?" Harper asks. "It's a Thursday night. Don't you have early class tomorrow?"

Damn it. Not that lucky, I guess.

"Sporting event."

"Wait..." Her blue eyes give me an assessing stare.

"The only thing happening tonight is the hockey game. There's no way you'd be going to *this* game."

"Why aren't you going?" I deflect.

"I have my big presentation to get ready for tomorrow for the ed school. I'll see Marcus tomorrow after. But you didn't answer my question."

Crap. I knew better than to let that skate by her.

"Troy invited me."

"And does he know your history with a certain Boston player?"

I nod.

"Oh, this is good. Troy is going to level Kyle! I wish I could go."

"Your presentation is more important than the game."

"Besides,"—Harper waves me off—"with the playoffs coming up, I'll have more games to go to."

"They haven't made it in yet."

Even though they are in the top of their conference and will likely get an automatic spot, anything could happen in the next few weeks.

The team got off to a strong start after the holidays. I hated that right when I got back, Troy left.

The life of an athlete. Something I'll have to get used to, like I've found myself getting used to other things about him.

The way butterflies swarm my stomach every time I even think about him. The way I dream about his smile. Or the way his eyes light up when he figures out the answer to a problem.

I shouldn't be so enamored with him. But I am.

And that is very, *very* bad.

Even though it feels like so much more than that one simple word. It doesn't carry the true weight of what we mean to one another.

"Have fun and tell Troy I said hi! And give Marcus a kiss for me!"

"Not happening, you nerd!" I grab my purse from the counter and turn to leave. "Bye, Harper! Don't wait up."

"Oh, I won't."

Bypassing my car for the night, I wait for the bus to take me to the arena. I'm stressed enough as it is. I don't need to add waiting in traffic to the list.

A packed bus pulls up. San Diego is known for its hockey program. Players from all across the country want to play here. I cram my way on as we pull out toward the arena.

The closer we get, the more my nerves start to amp up. It's not that I don't like hockey. I do. But Kyle turned me off of the sport when he left me high and dry.

And because I know Kyle is here, I'm nervous.

It's hard to support a game when one person made you hate it.

I'll do whatever I can do support Troy, though. Because he's worth it.

The bus pulls up to the arena and students spill out. Even outside, the tension is palpable.

Boston and SDU are two of the top teams in the country. And I want nothing more than for the Sand Sharks to pull out a win.

I follow everyone inside, getting my ticket scanned and finding my seat.

I give a warm smile to the older couple sitting next to me. Most college students sit in the upper deck, but seeing as how Troy got me this ticket, I'm close to the glass.

"Hi." The older woman smiles up at me.

"Hi." I drop into the seat next to her, my gaze focusing on the ice below.

Swarms of red and white cover the arena. Energy is pulsing in the rink as the team is on the ice warming up.

I spy #22 on the ice. Troy makes this look easy. He's flying over the ice, deftly handling the puck with his stick.

It shouldn't be as sexy as it is—watching him play this game. But he's good. There's a reason he was recruited out of high school.

Something my ex never was. If only I could tell him that.

Troy skates over to where I'm sitting. Flipping his visor up, he gives me a wave before looking at the people next to him. Heat blooms on my cheeks.

I haven't felt this way in so long. I love that even when he's on the ice, he's giving me attention.

My wave back is shy before he's off to continue warm-up.

"Oh my God. Are you Angie?" the woman next to me asks.

"I am."

A smile lights up her face, deepening the lines around her eyes. I don't even need to hear what she says next to know who this is.

"We've heard so much about you. I'm Sutton, Troy's mother."

Oh no. Oh no, no, no.

This can't be happening.

"And this is his father." She leans back, indicating to the man next to her.

Troy is the spitting image of him. Same dark brown hair. Brown eyes, so dark, they're almost black. He has more wrinkles around his eyes, but the smile he gives me is kind.

So unlike every story I've heard growing up about this man.

"It's nice to meet you. I'm Derek."

"Hi." I take his extended hand. "Angie."

"So you're the young lady we've heard so much about."

"Uhh…"

I'm turning into a bumbling idiot around these people. What exactly has Troy told them about me?

Do they know who I am? Who my dad is?

There is no way they'd be smiling at me like they are if they knew my dad was Alex Young.

Could this be any more of a nightmare?

"Don't worry, all good things," his mom tells me. "We're so thankful you're helping him with his studies. It's very important to us that he graduates before going pro. Playing professional sports only lasts so long."

"I'm glad I'm able to help him." I wish I had something to clear my parched throat. My voice sounds different to my own ears. As if I weren't stressed enough about coming to the game tonight, I'm meeting Troy's parents. "I know he wants to make you two proud."

"I don't know why he'd be worried about that. We're already proud of him. No matter what happens." No truer words from a mother.

"Sutton, let her be. I'm sure she doesn't want to spend the night with you talking her ear off."

"Oh, it's okay!" I squeak out.

Get it together, Angela. You're acting like a crazy person right now.

It's at that moment the opposing team skates out onto the ice.

Maroon and gold jerseys clash with the red and white of SDU. The team name is splashed across the front.

Boston Gophers.

I wish I couldn't pick Kyle out, but there he is. A head

taller than everyone on his team. There's a cockiness to him that I can sense even from here.

He hasn't changed a bit.

I don't miss the way Troy skates by him during warm-ups. No doubt he's assessing him, seeing if he can psych him out.

It makes me fall for him that much more.

"I really hope we beat them tonight," Sutton says from next to me.

Me too.

And I wouldn't mind if the captain takes someone out.

I'd love it in fact.

I can't wait for this game to start.

Chapter Twenty-Two

TROY

"Why the fuck are you so happy?" Marcus yells at me, shooting the puck over to me. I slide it across the ice, hitting the back of the net.

"Why can't I be happy that the game is tonight?"

"Dude, you're never this happy to be playing hockey. It's unnatural."

It's true. With the stress of my grades and the fear of losing my position on the team, it was touch and go there for a while. But now? Angie and hockey are my main focus.

"See! There's that smile again."

"Fuck off, Wizard."

Except my eyes keep drifting over to where Angie is sitting. With my parents. I feel a twinge of guilt that I didn't tell her, but I knew she wouldn't come if she knew they'd be here.

Is it so bad to want my girlfriend to meet my parents?

All I know is that I want to have the game of my life tonight.

Sue me; I want to show off for her.

And maybe lay out her ex.

"Alright boys, circle up!" Coach Morris calls out to us. "Tonight's going to be a hard one. Boston is one of the top-ranked schools in the country. But we're better than they are. And with Tanner back, they'll be gunning for a win."

"Tanner. What an ass," someone mumbles.

If only he knew the half of it.

My eyes flit to Angie's. She's chatting away with my mom. But it's like she feels my eyes on her and she turns to face me.

Even from here, I can sense her nerves.

I know she doesn't want to bump into her ex. My only hope is to lay him out on the ice.

Scouts are at the game tonight. With the end of the season fast approaching, they're at more and more games. I know I don't have a reputation for being a dirty player, but I don't want one game to ruin my shot at the pros.

I've gone through the motions during pregame. I blink and we're getting ready to line up to start the game.

"You okay?" Marcus asks.

"Oh, I'm good."

Kyle skates up to center ice as I meet him.

"Hope you're ready for a long game. We're going to embarrass you tonight on your home ice," he chirps.

Oh yeah. His trash talk is going to make this even better.

The puck is dropped and I take it with ease before passing it off to Isaac.

"Long game? Might want to check yourself." I wink at him before skating off down the ice.

He's at my skates, stick clashing with mine.

"Watch your back, Hollins. I'll get you before you know it."

"Try me."

From the minute the game starts, Kyle does nothing but trash talk. I don't get a clean shot against him. Not without pulling a penalty.

Marcus and I get shots on goal, but Boston's goalie is good. Undoubtedly the best in the country.

He guards the crease with an ease that comes naturally. It makes me hate the guy that all of our shots get blocked.

"Fuck!" I slam my stick against the boards at our last shift change of the first period.

"Easy, man. We'll get there." Marcus passes over my water bottle as I watch Isaac draw a dumb penalty and get two minutes in the box.

"Really?"

We're down a man, letting Boston score an easy goal.

"Damn it!"

I'm pissed. The last thing I want is to get down against this team. Especially when we skate off the ice and I get a scathing look from Kyle.

"There'll be more of that all night, baby. All night."

"I really want to beat him," I tell Marcus.

"Why do you want to beat him so badly? We're used to dicks like him."

I follow him into the locker room for intermission.

"That's Angie's ex."

"Shit. Are you serious?"

I nod, dropping down onto the wooden bench.

"Okay, that makes me want to cream him."

"Not before me." No one gets to do that before me.

"Not the end of the period we wanted, but we're only down by one. Still plenty of hockey left to play. Boston is a good team. We need to clean up some mistakes, not let easy penalties get the better of us."

"Sorry, Coach," Isaac tells everyone. "I'll do better."

"We all need to tighten up," Coach confirms. "Not just you."

"We got this, Coach. No way are we going to let these guys come in and beat us on our home ice!" I pipe up.

"That's right. Go out there and show those Gophers what happens when they mess with Sand Sharks!"

Everyone is fired up as we head back out to start the second period. Kyle wins the face-off this time, but I'm able to easily take the puck away from him.

Our guys are there to set up the play as I skate down the ice in the direction toward their net.

Marcus is on my left as I pass the puck off. Boston's D is setting up to block the play, but I slip between the two of them as Marcus sends the puck my way. Pulling back, I send it toward the back of the net. There's a small gap between the goalie's glove and the cross bar.

Watching the puck slide in, I cheer as the lamp lights up and the horn blares. The home stands erupt.

"We need more of that magic!" Marcus claps me on the helmet.

"All you, Wizard!"

This is why the two of us make such a good team. We know where the other is going to be on the ice. It's that intuition that makes playing with him so damn fun.

We head back to the bench as the second line takes the ice. It's a grind for the rest of the period. Neither team scores again, but thankfully we've cleaned up the silly mistakes.

My body aches as we start the third period. Boston is a hard-hitting team and hasn't been holding back.

Time is winding down in the game. The last thing I want is for this to go into overtime. And to not get a chance to take out my anger on Kyle.

An offsides call might give me my opportunity. Marcus

takes the face-off at their end of the ice, both Kyle and I waiting to grab the puck.

"Think you're going to win tonight?" Kyle is elbowing me in the side.

"Newsflash, idiot. Score is tied." I push right back on him.

"Not for long."

"We're on your end. Better watch your back."

Marcus wins the face-off and I grab the puck. Spinning away from Kyle, I skate back with the puck and wait for Marcus and Randy to set up the play.

Kyle is coming at me full speed. Before he can get a hit in, I shoot the puck to Marcus and brace for what comes next. I shift enough to miss Kyle and watch as he collides with the boards.

"Oooh," echoes through the arena before the fans explode with cheers. No doubt Marcus or Randy scored, but my eyes are on the player on the ice.

"That was a cheap shot!" He's yelling to the ref. "He goaded me into the boards!"

"I didn't even touch you!" I shout to him. I can't hide the grin on my face. It's even better than I imagined. He's spitting mad, trying to plead his case to get a major penalty on me.

"Fuck you, Hollins!" He skates by me, and it takes everything in me not to push him back down.

With less than a minute left, I ignore him and focus on finishing the game. Boston pulls their goalie to get an extra player, but to no avail.

SDU wins, 2-1. It was a hard-fought victory, made even sweeter knowing I put Angie's ex in his place.

"Enjoy that flight back to Boston!" I shout across the ice to Kyle. If looks could kill, I'd be six feet under.

And I don't mind one bit. My eyes scan the crowd and

lock on to Angie's. She's shaking her head at me, but the smile belies her true feelings.

I know Angie is as happy as I am that we won. Nothing feels better than a win. Especially one that has my parents and Angie in attendance.

By the time I'm done showering and changing, the locker room has almost cleared out. I wave goodbye and head out.

And there is Angie, lingering outside the locker room. I'm surprised to see her here with my parents close by.

"Hey."

"I think I'm owed something." She waggles her eyebrows at me.

"Owed something?"

"My hat. I didn't see a hat trick tonight, Troy."

Laughter burbles out of me. I fish her red hat out of my bag and pull it over her head.

"Guess I need to try harder next time."

"Mmm." She presses up onto her toes and gives me a quick kiss. "That pass to Marcus where Kyle tried to take you out? I loved it."

"All for you, Ang."

I want to dip her in my arms and lay one on her, but I can't.

"Got time to say hi to your parents?"

Mom comes over in the tunnel, my dad behind her.

"Hi, Mom."

"That was a great game, Troy. I was so nervous you wouldn't pull off the win."

I give my mom a hug. "Thanks for the confidence."

"Oh, we knew you'd win." Dad is laughing as he wraps an arm around Mom. "You wouldn't want to disappoint Angie here."

"Dad," I whisper-hiss at him.

"Sorry, sorry." He laughs, throwing his hands up. "Uncool of me, I know. But we had a great time."

"We did," Angie confirms. "I'm glad I got to know your parents."

"Yeah?" I look at her to see if she's serious. The warm smile there tells me she's not lying. I breathe a sigh of relief.

Maybe if she sees the type of man my dad truly is, it'll pave the way to making this thing between us more permanent.

"I know you two will want to celebrate, so why don't you come over for breakfast tomorrow, okay? Bring Angie." Mom clasps my cheek and drops a kiss there.

A warmth blooms in my chest. This is why I love being so close to home. I love my family as much as Angie loves hers. Sutton is the only mom I've ever known. She married my dad when I was five, so I don't really remember a life without her in it.

She and my dad have done everything in their power to support not only my hockey career, but my sister's too. All I want to do is make them proud.

"We'll be there." I give her an extra tight hug. "Love you, Mom."

She lets me go and Dad pulls me in close, whispering into my ear. "Love you, son. Don't let her go."

"What?" My brows furrow as I look at him. Can he see what I'm feeling for Angie?

She's hugging my mom goodbye.

"Alright. Time to go." Mom pulls Dad away before he can get another word in.

"Sooo…" Angie trails off as my parents leave the arena. It's dark back here in this part of the rink. Just the two of us. "Looks like I met your parents."

"Are you okay with that? I'm sorry I didn't tell you."

"They're great, Troy. Really."

"Yeah?"

"Yeah."

"Then do you want to go to breakfast with them tomorrow?"

"Sure."

"That easy?" I ask, staring down at her.

Angie nods, stepping closer to me. "That easy. Because I want to talk about how well you played tonight."

She walks her fingers up my chest and grasps my chin in her hands. Her eyes darken with lust.

Oh yeah. This is what I was hoping would happen tonight. I back her up against the wall. Glancing in both directions, I confirm we're the only two here. With the locker room behind me, I know there's still a chance someone could come out at any minute.

I lick a path up her neck before whispering, "I played for you tonight."

Angie's hands fist in my suit jacket. Coach's requirements—no looking like slobs at the game.

"I know you did." Her head tilts to the side, letting me have better access.

"I liked knowing you were in the stands."

"Watching you play made me…" Her words trail off.

"Made you what?" I nibble on the pulsing vein in her neck.

I think I have a pretty good idea what the game did to her tonight.

"Hot. I'm so fucking turned on right now, Troy, I don't know what I'll do."

A door opens behind us, breaking the trance I'm in.

"Meet me at my car in ten minutes."

Chapter Twenty-Three

ANGIE

Anticipation is going to overwhelm me. It's been twenty minutes since Troy told me to meet him by his Jeep.

I'm pacing back and forth, waiting for him, when my phone buzzes in my pocket. I'm half expecting it to be him, but it's not. My heart sinks at the name lighting up my phone.

Scanning the parking lot and seeing it's still empty, I slide to answer.

"Hey Dad."

"Angela. I haven't talked to you this week. Just wanted to check in and see how your last semester of college is starting out."

"It's good, Dad."

"Good? That's it? I haven't talked to you in a week and that's all I get?"

I laugh, trying to break up the tightness in my chest. It's getting harder and harder to keep the truth from him. Instead of picking up when he calls, I send him to voicemail.

"Sorry. I'm just focusing on my schoolwork. Of course, Harper keeps dragging me out, so I'm getting a nice social life too."

His laugh rings through the phone. "Don't sound so upset by that. Colin would be so disappointed you're not breaking any rules."

"I'm sure he would be." The king of breaking the rules, Colin James. My godfather.

Yet, here I am. Breaking the biggest rule of all. One that I see exiting the arena now.

"Listen, Dad, I've got to go."

"Don't forget, we'll be visiting Grandma and Grandpa next month for their big anniversary."

"Uh-huh." I don't hear his words as I see a familiar figure heading toward me.

"Everything okay?"

"Great, fine. Love you."

I hang up before I hear anything else.

The look on Troy's face has me pushing the phone call from my mind.

Watching him play hockey might be the biggest aphrodisiac. I never remember it being like that with Kyle. Kyle was always a dick when he was on the ice. Watching Troy play is completely different.

There's an intelligence to the way he plays. He's smart. He doesn't make dumb moves. Sure, not everything was in their favor tonight, but Troy made smart plays to get them into the game.

Especially not flattening Kyle like I thought he would. He let him do that all on his own. The look on Kyle's face was worth it.

Absolutely priceless.

"What are you smiling about?"

"Thinking about how well you played tonight."

Troy lifts me into his arms and presses me against the metallic green side of his car. "How else does it make you feel?"

I grind down against his very obvious hard-on. "About the same as you."

"What are we going to do about it?"

"Why don't you let us into your car and we can take care of this…growing problem?"

"Fuck, Angie."

Troy clicks the remote, and the beep echoes across the parking lot. He sets me on my feet so I can get into the back seat as he crawls in behind me. It isn't the most spacious place to be. With his backpack on the floor and an empty water bottle, there's little room for our legs, and there's no way we can stretch out.

Troy must be reading my mind as he pulls me across the seats, settling me onto his lap. He claims my mouth with his.

The kiss is punishing. Hot need and desire swirl in the air around us. I dig my fingers into Troy's shoulders as I grind down on his cock. It is hitting every part of me that I want.

"I love how hot you are from watching me play."

I brush the hair out of Troy's face. "I could watch you play forever and I don't think it'd ever be enough."

"Fuck, Ang."

He kisses me again. Long, slow, lust-inducing kisses that have me so close to coming, I should be embarrassed.

"I could come like this."

"Do it." His voice is commanding. "Get yourself off."

Troy leans back against the seat, hands drifting under my sweatshirt. He tweaks my nipples as I do exactly as he says.

The windows start to fog. If anyone were to walk by, they'd know what is going on in here.

I couldn't care less. All I want is for Troy to get me off.

Right.

Fucking.

Now.

His cock tents the material of his black suit pants as I continue grinding down on him.

"So good."

"Fuck, Ang. C'mon. I want to see how I can get you off wearing all of your clothes."

"Mmm. I can feel how hard you are. How I make you feel."

His fist tightens in my hair, tilting my head to the side. "Are you thinking about what it would feel like if my dick were fucking you right now?"

"Oh God." His words are amping up my need. My belly is coiling tight as my clit rubs against the hard length in his pants. "I can't wait to feel you inside me."

"Gotta come like this first."

Troy arches up off the leather seat. We're dry humping like rabbits, trying to get off as quick as possible.

"Watching you tonight…gah!"

My orgasm slams into me. I throw my head back, barely missing the roof as I let out a scream.

I don't care who can hear me now. Let anyone walking by know just how incredible Troy is.

"Fuck. Watching you come like this is hot, Angie. So fucking hot."

Troy doesn't waste any time as he slides my leggings off my hips. I don't have more than a minute to catch my breath as he pushes the condom packet into my hand.

It's not the easiest of angles in the small space, but neither of us care as I roll the condom down his hard length. It's a frenzied moment, the two of us needing each other more than we care to admit.

Troy holds himself steady as I sink down on him. Feeling each inch as he fills me up.

I swivel my hips, taking him deeper. We move together. He swallows down every moan and gasp. I take every grunt and arch of his hips.

"Fuck, Angie." Troy's orgasm hits him and it takes me over with him. I squeeze out every last drop of his release as we come together.

The air is sticky with sex and heat. My pulse is racing as I come down from the high of being with Troy.

Emotions are threatening to overwhelm me as I'm held in Troy's embrace. Strong arms that keep me safe. That cherish me.

Love me.

I bite down on my lip to keep from crying out.

I love Troy. It's in everything he's done for me these last few months. The way we are when we're together.

Maybe this was why I fought him so hard in the beginning. Because I knew this thing between us would turn into so much more.

I never expected to fall in love with him. But I have. I've gone and done the one thing I said I couldn't do.

I fell in love with Troy Hollins.

Falling for Troy was easy. The hard part now?

Figuring out how to keep him.

Chapter Twenty-Four

ANGIE

"You know you didn't have to bring anything, right?" Troy tells me as we get out of his Jeep at his parents' house.

"And show up empty-handed?" I scoff. "Never."

Even though we only talked a little bit during the game, I still want to impress his parents.

"And you still wouldn't let me have a cinnamon roll on the drive over."

I swat the hand that is reaching toward the container.

"They're for breakfast."

"But I'm hungry," he whines with a pout.

"And we'll be eating soon." The front door opens and his mom is standing there.

"Thank God. I'm starving."

Troy darts up the porch and drops a kiss on Sutton's cheek.

"Your dad is finishing up breakfast. It's almost ready."

"Hopefully you don't have any of these." I hand over the tin of cinnamons rolls.

"These smell delish. You didn't have to make anything."

"I wanted to."

She gives me a warm smile. Her blonde hair is pulled back into a ponytail and she's wearing a pink sweater and jeans.

"That's so sweet of you, dear. C'mon. Let me grab you something to drink."

Sutton guides me into the house. It's a large, open floor plan with a living room that flows seamlessly into the kitchen. It's all modern whites and grays with hints of black throughout. The living room wall is decorated with more pictures than I can count.

"Would you like a mimosa, Angie?" Sutton asks.

"Sure. Is there anything I can do to help?"

Sutton waves my offer off. "You just relax. We're so happy you and Troy are here today."

"No Lydia?" Troy and his dad are at the stove, and I notice that Troy is nearly a head taller than Derek. He turns back from the stove, leaning against the marble countertop.

"Team has practice today."

"I'm sorry I can't meet her," I tell them, taking the drink Sutton hands me.

"She wishes she could meet you too." Sutton walks over to Troy and hands him a stack of plates and forks. "Set the table and show Angie around while we finish up."

"Okay, Mom."

He grabs another piece of bacon, munching as he walks.

I take the silverware on top and follow him to the table where we set it for the four of us.

"This feels weirdly domestic," Troy tells me.

"What, you didn't want to bring your girlfriend home to breakfast?"

Troy drops a kiss on my lips. "It feels like we've been doing this for a long time."

It does. A lot longer than we've been together. But this is only the second time I'm meeting his parents.

I set the last fork down and put my drink on the table. "C'mon. Show me around."

Troy grabs my hand and leads me down a hallway. One that is filled with more pictures.

"This picture is adorable." I stop, pointing to the gap-toothed kid in the picture as Troy drops his chin onto my shoulder.

"I think I was six then?"

Troy and a little girl are both standing on the ice in skates with their arms around each other.

"Is that your sister?"

"It is. I think it was a year after our parents got married."

"How'd they meet?"

The entire wall is filled with pictures. Troy as a kid. His parents. His sister. Family vacations. Hockey. Pictures of his dad coaching.

"I broke my arm as a kid, and Sutton was my nurse."

"And it was true love after that?"

Troy points to a picture on the wall. "They got married in Vegas a few months after they met."

"Really?"

The picture is of the four of them and another couple in what looks like a Vegas chapel. Elvis is standing behind them with Derek and Sutton kissing and the other two cheering.

"There is definitely a story here."

"My uncles, Jameson and Gunnar, were getting

EMILY SILVER

married. Elvis somehow convinced our parents to get married. Lydia and I thought it was the best idea ever. There was no looking back after that. We celebrated with milkshakes and swimming at the hotel pool."

"Sounds like a pretty good day."

Troy nods. "For a five-year-old? Yeah, it was the best day."

I spin in Troy's arms. "Do you ever see your birth mom?" I ask.

He shakes his head. "My mom cut out when I was little. She was a jersey chaser. I have no memory of her."

"None?"

He shakes his head, pressing a kiss to the inside of my wrist. "As far as I'm concerned, my mom is Sutton. She was always there for me. Still is."

"They both really love you."

His dad isn't the same guy I heard so much about growing up. It was evident at the hockey game. It's evident here on the walls of his parents' house.

"I hope they're proud of me."

"Hope?" Shock laces my voice. "Troy, I don't think I've ever met a pair of parents more proud of their son than you."

"Time to eat!" his dad calls out.

A smirk plays on Troy's lips as he rushes off to the dining room. I can't help but laugh at him.

"I'm starving!" he whines, dropping down into the seat across from his parents.

"You poor kid." Derek laughs at him.

Troy takes a heaping scoop of eggs and piles it on his plate.

"Save some for the rest of us," Sutton chides him, taking the platter from him as he passes it across the table.

"I'm a growing boy." He grins.

"You're twenty-two, Troy," Derek points out. "Growing boy, my ass."

"As long as you save some French toast for me," I tell Troy.

"How's your dad's organization going?" Derek asks, handing over a platter of French toast.

"Team Rainbow? How do you know about that?" I fork a piece of toast and drop it on my plate.

A sheepish look comes over his face. "I used to work with them at the high school when I was the coach."

"Really?"

"It was nothing big."

"Nothing big?" Sutton interjects. "I don't believe that for a second."

"I didn't do it for the recognition."

"Helping kids learn so they don't make your mistakes and creating a safe playing environment for everyone isn't nothing," she corrects him.

"It's the reason my dad started it." I smile at Derek.

To think, the man sitting across from me is the reason Team Rainbow started. The words—slurs, really—that he threw at my dad changed the course of his life. It's the entire reason he came out when he did. Why he started his charity after he retired.

Everything I was told about Derek Hollins growing up was false. There is nothing but love and kindness from them.

The words Derek said left a deep, emotional wound on him. When you get called the f-word? It leaves a mark. I only wish my dad could see this.

This person is someone my dad would like. Maybe.

At least it's that thought that gives me hope.

The same thought that carries us all through breakfast. Laughing and hearing stories about Troy growing up. The trouble that he and his sister used to get into. Stories of him with his uncles Jameson and Gunnar. Even though they aren't his real uncles, he's grown up with them in his life. Just like I did with all of my dad's old teammates.

I love hearing about it.

And all too soon, it's coming to an end.

"I need to get back for a workout." Troy throws his napkin on the table, resting his arm on the back of my chair.

"Need to work off breakfast?" I pat his stomach.

"Can't slack off now that the playoffs are almost here."

I help clear the table before we head out.

"Make sure you come back, okay?" Sutton pulls me into a hug.

"I will. Maybe we can do dinner after his next game?"

"Careful," Derek laughs. "Before you know it, she'll be wanting to sit with you at every game."

Sutton swats at him. "Well, it was good luck, wasn't it?"

"I plan on it."

"Keep up your good work, Troy. We love you." Derek hugs him, then Sutton pulls him in for a hug before they wave us off.

"Thanks for bringing me here today, Troy."

"Does that mean I'll get to bring you back?"

I nod, buckling my seatbelt. "You can bring me back anytime. I love your parents."

And I mean it.

I only hope Troy and I can have more days like this.

Chapter Twenty-Five

TROY

TROY

I'm picking you up in 15. Dress warm

ANGIE

What? Where are we going?

Be ready

Troy Hollins!

Down to 10

Why do I have to dress warm?

Because we're going out

It's February. It's too cold to do anything but stay inside

I thought you were a Colorado girl and could handle the cold

Why do you think I came to school in San Diego?

5 minutes…

Troy!

Are you ready?

If I say no, can we stay inside?

2 minutes

Fine. I'll be ready

That's my girl

"It's too cold to go to the beach!" Angie burrows deeper into my side. Her sweet perfume wafts over me. I never knew that it could be so calming, but every time I smell that sugary vanilla perfume, it reminds me of Angie, putting me at ease.

"You have my hoodie. You'll be fine. Besides, it's not that cold."

"Look!" She pulls the sleeve of said hoodie up. "Goose bumps, Troy. Goose bumps."

"Do you need me to keep you warm?" I wrap the blanket I brought with me around her shoulders.

"Yes."

Tucking the blanket around her, I drop down onto the sand and pull her with me, settling her between my legs.

Even though it's cooler than normal out tonight, people are scattered across the beach. Families are flying kites, and groups of what look like friends are huddled around bonfire pits.

Our spot near the lifeguard tower is quiet. The rush of

the tide coming in helps settle the overwhelming thoughts that have been starting to plague me these last few days.

"So why'd you bring me out here to freeze tonight?"

I wrap my arms closer around her, rubbing her arms to keep her warm.

"I needed a quiet place to think. To not be on campus and be talking about hockey or school and what might or might not happen this summer."

"Have you heard anything from the scouts that came?"

"Not yet. Still impressed with my game, but no hint as to which way they'll be leaning."

"I don't know how you do it. That kind of limbo would make me crazy."

"I'm trying not to think about it, but it's hard."

"Why didn't you tell me you were worried?"

"That's why I brought you out here with me, didn't I?"

Over the course of these last few months, Angie has become my go-to person. I don't know when it happened, exactly, but hers is the one opinion I seek out over anyone else's.

Probably around the time I fell in love with her.

Because that is exactly what has happened.

I fell in love with the one person I shouldn't have fallen in love with. Getting to keep her is a completely different story.

"What do you think is going to happen with the draft?" Angie's voice is quiet, barely heard over the breeze coming in off the water. It pulls me from my errant train of thought. The sun is almost at the horizon. Orange streaks across the ocean.

I blow out a breath. "I just hope to be drafted by any team."

"Any team?" she asks, shifting in my arms to face me.

"I mean, not Nashville. The Knights are the worst team in the league. Bunch of dirty players."

"Okay, so not Nashville. Do you have a team you'd want to play for?"

I drop my chin onto her shoulder, contemplating that. "I haven't given much thought to it."

"Why not?"

"Because I didn't want to fail out of college and have these teams realize what a failure I am and then not pick me up."

Angie spins, dropping onto her knees between my legs. I look up into her big, beautiful, brown eyes. "You listen to me, Troy Hollins."

"Uh-oh. Full name."

Her lips quirk up at the corner. "Because I want you to listen to me."

"Okay."

"You are not a failure. You would have failed if you didn't come to me. Most people don't want to ask for help, but you did."

"And thankfully you said yes." I try to laugh off the seriousness of the moment. "Because we're here now."

Graduation is coming on sooner than I want. Before, I wanted to be done and picked up by any team that would have me. My dad and mom wanted to make sure I got an education because hockey wouldn't last forever.

I was angry with them when I first came to SDU. Hockey was everything to me. I wanted to be in the big leagues. To bypass college altogether.

Now, I can't help but wonder if it was all part of some bigger plan for me. Because if I left early, I wouldn't have met Angie.

Slotting her into my life plans has been easy. Wherever I end up, I want her by my side.

"Where do you want to end up?" she asks me again.

"Colorado. I've wanted to be a Black Diamond since high school."

"Denver. Interesting choice."

"Why's that interesting?" I nudge her side.

"I'm hoping to end up in Denver. Fancy that."

"Huh. I had no idea," I say with a grin.

"What do you think would happen if we both end up there?" she asks. "Do you think we'll still be together?"

"That's up to you."

She spins in my arms, kneeling between my legs. "Why me?"

I guess it's time to put everything on the line. Not like we haven't talked about the future before, but it's always been in general terms—something so far away, we didn't really have to think about it.

Now? Now it's here. It's coming whether we want it to or not. I want her to know exactly how I see my future.

With her in it.

"Angie, I love you. More than I ever thought possible. But this thing between us? There's a very big bump in the road if we plan on staying together."

Tears gather in her eyes as her shoulders slump forward. "My dads."

"Yes."

"I know."

Tilting her chin up with my knuckle, I force her to look at me. "I want to be with you, Angie. This future I'm thinking about? I want you there with me. But I don't want to come between you and your family."

Her lip quivers, and it damn near breaks my heart.

"I love you too, Troy. I love you and I want to be with you so badly it hurts. But I don't know how to do that. How do I tell the two most supportive parents there are that I am with the son of someone who caused them so much pain?"

Those are the words I wanted to hear so badly from her. I wish they weren't fraught with so much emotion.

"Why don't we figure it out together?"

"You make it sound so easy." Her voice breaks, and I pull her into my arms.

"If it means I get to be with you, I'd walk through the gates of hell and back."

"Okay, I don't think it'll be that bad. Well, maybe."

The last rays of sun hit the beach, and it's then I decide to break up the heaviness of the moment. Lifting Angie into my arms, I run toward the water.

"If you drop me in this water, Troy, I will kick your ass!" Angie shrieks in my ear. "That is a promise!"

"Oh yeah?" I make like I'm going to drop her, but catch her before I do.

"That's just mean." Her laughter eases everything inside of me. "I take back everything I said before."

"What part of it?"

Angie wraps her legs and arms around me like a koala. "The part where I said I loved you."

I shake my head. "You can't take that back."

"If you drop me in this water, I will."

"Even if I make you hot chocolate and spend all night warming you up?"

She rolls her head, as if debating it. "I could be convinced."

"Then how about we head back to your place, and I can make good on that promise?"

She bites down on her lip and nods. "I'm ready for you to warm me up."

I don't set Angie down as I walk back toward the parking lot.

It's been the perfect day. One I hope to continue with Angie for a long, long time. The two of us loving each other.

Forever, really.

As long as the two of us can figure out a way forward.

Together.

Chapter Twenty-Six

TROY

"Are you always this slow?" Angie laments. "I'm still cold."

"Are you always this impatient?"

I grab my bag from the back seat and lock my Jeep.

"When I want hot chocolate? Yeah." Her eyes are playful as she opens the back door to her building.

"That's all you want?"

"What else could I possibly need?" There's a skip to her step as she tries to run away from me.

"Not so fast." I throw her over my shoulder and bolt up the stairs. "You're not getting away from me that quickly."

"Troy! Put me down!" Her laughter echoes around the stairwell as I open the door to her floor.

The hallways are quiet as I walk through the maze to her apartment.

"Uhh, Angie?" I stop short of her front door. I recognize the faces hovering in the hallway. And I certainly don't miss the way they're glaring at us.

"What?" There's still a playfulness to her voice.

Not for much longer. I set her down and step away

from her. It's like a chasm is opening up between us already.

"Oh, shit," she whispers. The color drains from her face. "Shit, shit, shit."

"Angela," the tall man with brown but graying hair says.

The way he says her name is a way only a parent can say it. One when you're about to get in trouble.

"What are you doing here, Dad?" There's a panic in her voice. One that I feel even from three feet away.

"Don't you remember? The anniversary party is this weekend."

"Shit. I forgot."

Angie's gaze flicks to mine before returning to the group of people in front of us.

"I guess there's a few things you forgot." He crosses his arms. The way his biceps flex under his shirt has me shaking. This is Angie's dad, the famed Denver quarterback?

Everything I ever heard about him was what a great person he was. I guess that doesn't extend to people dating his daughter.

"So you decided to surprise me and show up at my door? What if I was busy?"

"Apparently you are," the woman behind Alex whispers.

"Marley, not now," the man next to Alex hisses. "Why don't we take this inside?"

Finally. The first voice of reason.

Whatever happens, I don't want to risk anyone walking out on this…shit show.

Because that's exactly what it feels like.

With Angie and me at the center.

22

Angie

I swallow back the bile that's rising in my throat. When I woke up today, this was the furthest thing from my mind.

I was just going to be working on a paper and enjoying a night with Troy.

Coming home to find my dads, aunt, and uncle on my doorstep? I never thought this would happen.

Troy and I only just made the decision to tell them about us. It's not like we had any time to figure out the best way to do it. But finding out like this? It's even worse.

"Angela Brooks-Young. What in the world is going on here?" Dad asks. His voice is calm. So calm, I've never seen him like this.

The silence is deafening.

"I…"

I have no words. Anxiety and dread are pooling in my gut. There's no way this is going to turn out okay for us.

"Why don't you tell us what is going on here…with Mr. Hollins?" Dad quirks a brow at me.

Growing up, I always loved that I looked just like my dad. But now, I hate seeing that anger directed at me.

"You obviously know who this is."

"But what are you doing with him?" he snaps. Anger laces his voice.

"I think you know." Anything other than the truth would insult him at this point.

"You know what his father is like. What he did."

That draws my eyes up to his. Whatever I'm feeling

turns to anger at that moment. "You're basing your judgment on him from an opinion that is twenty years old."

"A leopard doesn't change his spots, Angela."

"He did. I've met him and—"

"You what?" He's back to the eerie calm.

I straighten my spine. I'm not backing down from this conversation. "I went to Troy's hockey game and sat with his parents. They are lovely people if you'd get to know them."

"So you're into hockey players again? What happened about not dating them after everything that happened with Kyle?"

I fight the eye roll. If I want to keep this productive, I have to be the mature one here. "Troy isn't like other hockey players. Maybe if you would sit down and talk with him instead of judging him before we're in the door, you'd see that."

Dad shakes his head. He's about as done with this conversation as I am.

"Mr. Young—" Troy starts, but Dad is quick to stop him.

"I'm not done with Angela yet."

"Dad. Can you please just calm down?"

"Uh-oh," Aunt Marley whispers, eyes flying to my dad.

"Calm down? I think I'm being as calm as the situation warrants."

"How am I the more mature one in this conversation?" I shout.

"Angie…" Troy whispers, but I ignore him.

"Aren't you the one that talks about being open and inclusive to everyone from all walks of life? Or is that all just talk to you?"

"It's different when you know someone."

"You don't know him though!" I shake my head. "Why are you being like this?"

"Are you really going to throw away your family for him?" Dad nods his head toward Troy.

The floor drops out from under me. "What?"

I couldn't have heard him right. There's no way my dad would say those words. All over some guy?

Except it's not just *some guy*.

It's Troy.

The man I love. I don't think that will help me in this situation.

"Alex," Pops cuts through. "I think we all need to take a minute to cool off."

Dad is seething. If fire came out of his ears, it wouldn't surprise me.

"I'm going to leave," Troy whispers, backing toward the door. His face tells me everything I need to know.

"Please don't."

"I can't stay."

I reach for him, but he shakes me off. My breath catches in my chest. Everything is unraveling before my eyes. "Don't leave like this, Troy."

"I'll call you later." He gives me a weak smile and is out the door. It shuts softly behind him, but it echoes in the quiet of the apartment.

"Angela. Why don't—"

I don't know who says it, as the rage that's brewing inside me takes over everything.

"Leave."

"Sweetheart. Let's just take a minute and talk things over." This time, it's Aunt Marley.

"No." Tears are streaming down my face. "I can't talk to any of you right now."

"Just as well." Dad stands from the couch and heads to

the door. "I don't think it would be a productive conversation."

He leaves without another word. Aunt Marley and her husband follow him, but Pops remains.

I brush angry tears away. My heart is cracking inside my chest.

"Give him a few days to calm down. It just took him by surprise is all."

"And you think this is how I wanted you to find out about Troy?" I turn to face him. His face is sympathetic. Growing up, he was always the calming influence of the two of them. "Pops, I…"

"I know, sweetheart." He wraps me into a hug. "I know. I'll talk to him."

I want him to stay. To wrap me in his arms and protect me from the world like he did when I was a kid. His hugs–*their hugs*–always fixed everything.

And now, I can't even think about it without anger and pain mixing together.

Because with one swift move, everything in my life has changed.

No Troy.

No parents.

Nothing.

What is a girl supposed to do?

Chapter Twenty-Seven

ANGIE

"Are you sure it's okay if I come tonight?" Harper asks from the passenger seat of my car.

"If you don't, I might be subject to killing one of my dads. And that's the last thing any of us needs."

I haven't spoken to anyone in my family since everything happened. Four long days. I've skipped every single class—a first for me since I started college. Troy's been calling, but I haven't been able to pick up the phone. Harper is the only person I've seen. I'm too heartbroken to do anything but stay in my room.

I don't know how to forgive my dad while trying to keep Troy in my life. But when I got a call from my grandma, telling me in no uncertain terms that I had to be at the party, Harper got my ass in gear.

A shower. A little makeup to look presentable. And a simple black dress. Not much more I could muster the energy for.

"Okay, there will be no killing tonight. I don't want to visit you in prison."

That gets a laugh out of me. "Fine. But you are not to leave my side."

"Are you sure you don't want to call Troy?" Harper asks as I pull into the long driveway where my grandparents live.

"No. The last thing I need is to bring him into the lion's den and subject the man I love to people who hate him."

"Oh, Ang." Harper gives me a pitiful look. "I wish I knew how you felt about him."

I suck in a deep breath, willing the tears not to come. "It doesn't matter how I feel. Right now, all that matters is I get through tonight without dealing with my dads."

"That might be hard."

Harper points to the front door as I park the car. Pops is standing outside, almost like he's awaiting our arrival.

"I thought he was the voice of reason." Harper unclicks her seatbelt and opens her door.

"Yeah, but tonight, I'm not feeling very reasonable."

Pops stays where he is as Harper and I walk toward him.

"Harper. It's lovely to see you." His voice is calm, steady. "How has school been this year for you?"

"Uhh,"—Harper looks back at me, like she's not quite sure what to make of this conversation—"good. I'm going to go get us some drinks. You okay?"

I nod to her, pulling my jacket tighter around me.

"Were you out here making sure I didn't bring Troy to the party?" Bitterness laces my tone.

"That's not fair."

"What, like it's fair how Dad treated Troy?" I scoff. "He treated him like the scum of the earth."

"He was taken aback, that's all."

"So he's come to his senses then?"

234

"Well…" He scrubs the back of his neck.

The tension on his face is obvious. Bags sit under his blue eyes. My guess is he's been doing nothing but worrying these last few days.

"That's a no." I brush by him into the house.

"Angela." His tone stops me. His teacher tone, as I called it growing up. I used to hate it when he used it on me. It meant I was in trouble. "Give him a little grace. He's struggling."

"Like the grace he gave me when he said it was Troy or my family?"

"He didn't mean it."

"It seemed like he did." My lip quivers. Damn it. The last thing I want to do is start crying now. I only wanted to make it through the night without issue.

"Carter, go help the caterers. Make sure they know where the food needs to go."

Grandma appears in the doorway.

"Marley was helping with that."

"I asked you."

He mutters something under his breath as he goes inside. It shouldn't give me as much joy as it does, seeing him get flustered by his own mother. But it does.

"Are you okay, dear?" Grandma pulls me into a hug. The smell of her rose perfume helps to calm my racing nerves.

"No. Not even in the ballpark of being okay."

"Don't you mean hockey rink?" Her eyes glitter behind her black cat-eye glasses.

"Grandma!"

"What?" She shrugs a shoulder as the colorful shawl she wears slides down her arm to her elbow. "I can form my own opinions on things. And I happen to disagree with your dads."

"You do?"

She nods, grabbing two glasses of champagne from a passing waiter. "I told them as such and was told I have no idea what I'm talking about."

I gulp down the entire glass in one go. I wasn't planning on drinking tonight, but Harper and I can get a rideshare home if need be.

"Of course you don't. Dad knows everything."

Grandma stops me in the hallway. Their house is big. An old Spanish-style house with tiled floors. Two staircases wrap around the entry with a vintage chandelier hanging over the space. Voices from the living room at the back of the house float toward us.

The table behind her has pictures of the entire family. The one I loved so much catches my eye. I'm sitting on my dad's shoulders after he won his first Super Bowl. Pops is at his side as confetti rains down over us.

I don't remember much from that day except the confetti. But I loved that picture. The one of us as a family. Now it tugs at my heart, thinking of my dad's words to me.

Would he really disown me because of Troy?

"C'mon, darling. No being sad tonight. We're celebrating our sixtieth wedding anniversary."

I sigh and let her drag me to the back where the party is happening. The living room opens to the dining room and kitchen. Everyone is hovering near the food that is being passed around.

People I recognize and don't recognize are here. My brother is sitting on the couch, his nose buried in a book. Harper is beside him.

I dodge the familiar faces of my aunts and uncles and head for them. There's no one else around them. Just how I want it.

"You doing okay?" Harper asks as I sit down on the

opposite side of my brother.

"I heard you screwed up big time." Nick doesn't bother looking up from the pages of his book.

"Nice to see you too, bro."

Harper passes me another glass of champagne. "You need this more than I do."

"Can I have a sip?" Nick asks, looking up.

"Oh, that's just what I need. Dad getting mad at me for giving you alcohol."

Nick snickers as another voice cuts into the conversation. "You are not giving your brother alcohol."

"Uncle Colin." I jump up and give him a quick hug. "I was doing no such thing."

"Even though I'm going to college and should experience it in a controlled environment before I get a taste at a frat party."

"Would you even go to a frat party?" Colin asks him.

"Maybe."

"That's a no," I tell him.

"How are ya, kid?" Colin asks. "How's the last semester going?"

Nick snorts behind me. "Wrong thing to ask."

"Nick," I hiss at him.

"Leave your sister alone." Harper swats at him.

"Going that well, huh?"

My godfather still looks as fit as ever. He didn't play as long as my dad, but still looks like he could suit up in a game of football if he needed to. And even with gray streaks through his hair, his face is still young and playful. He's always been this way.

It's why I love him so much. He never lets anything get him down. He and my Aunt Peyton were always people I could turn to when I needed them.

I don't know why I didn't think of asking for their

advice sooner. Maybe it would've prevented this situation from happening at all.

"It's fine. Semester will be over soon."

"And then you'll be back with us in Denver."

"Yup." I pop the *p*. Sarcasm is heavy. The very last thing I want to do now is go back to Denver.

"Did I miss something?" This time, Colin looks confused.

"Angela. Nick." Dad barely looks at me, addressing Nick. "Your grandpa is going to give a welcome toast. We'd like for you two to be there for it."

"Whatever you say, Dad." I give him a sickly sweet smile that twists his face up in annoyance.

"Can we please put aside this…situation for the night?"

"Situation?" Is he serious with this? "You threatening to disown me is more than a situation."

"Angela." He rubs his forehead, like I'm the source of the problem. "Please."

"Okay, I'm definitely missing something," Colin interjects.

"Angie is dating Derek Hollins's son," Nick tells him as he stands.

"Nick. You are not helping the 'situation'!" I shout at him.

"What? He asked."

Nick shrugs a shoulder and heads into the kitchen. Sometimes I hate how literal my brother can be. He is a genius—certified, at that. He could have already graduated from college if my dads didn't want him to have a more normal life.

At the rate he's going, he'll be able to finish grad school by the time he's twenty. If only he used that big brain of his to keep his mouth shut.

"Wait, seriously?" Uncle Colin asks, eyes flitting

between me and my dad. "You're shitting me?"

Both of us glare at him.

"Okay, when you both do that, it's weird." Colin turns his eyes to me. "When I told you to break the rules a little, I didn't mean this."

"Why is who Angie chooses to love that big of a deal?" Harper shouts. "Troy is the perfect man for her and cares about her. So what if you and his dad don't get along?"

I wince, waiting for the words to hit my dad. He is not going to be happy.

"I'm sorry...love?"

"Oh shit. I made things worse, didn't I?" Harper asks, regret written on her face.

"It's not helping, no."

"You're in love with him?" Dad asks again.

"Yes, I am."

"How did this happen?" Colin asks.

"Are the details really important?" I want to shake him or tell him to butt out of this conversation, but it'd do me no good. "Whether I love him or not, you're not going to approve."

"You've got that right," Dad huffs out. Everything about his posture is angry. Angry at me. Angry at Troy. Angry at Harper for dropping the "l" bomb.

"I don't know why I bothered coming tonight." I pass Harper my half-empty glass of champagne. I don't need it anymore. It's turning to cement in my stomach.

"You're a part of the family and we're celebrating."

"Oh, now I'm part of the family when it suits you?"

"Angela—"

I hold up a hand. "Save it, Dad. I came tonight because Grandma asked me to, but it was a mistake. It seems you can't talk about this rationally, so I'm going to go."

"You can't leave before the toast."

I throw my hands up in the air. "What's the point in celebrating their love when I won't get a chance at my own love story? You've ruined that."

"Angie—" he tries again.

"No, Dad. You're the one in the wrong here. I love Troy. He is kind, and caring, and sweet, and protects me. He is just like his dad. You have some antiquated notion of who he is based on the person he was twenty years ago. You're wrong. And until you can see that, I can't talk to you."

"So you're choosing him over your family?" Colin asks.

"No. Because Troy won't let me choose him over my family. As much as he loves me, he doesn't want to come between us."

"It's time for the toast," Pops says in a loud whisper as he steps over to us. I look behind him, seeing almost every eye turned in our direction.

Great.

"I'll see myself out." I grab Harper's hand and drag her past the curious onlookers.

"Sweetheart." Grandma is there, waiting for me. "You don't have to leave."

"Yes I do." I turn back to look at my dads. Neither of them are looking at me, but at the ground. Pops is clearly trying to talk to Dad, but I can't hear what they're saying from here. "Until they can realize I can make my own choices on who I love, I can't be here. I don't want to take away from your night."

And celebrating their love when I just lost mine?

I can't do it.

It cracks my heart a little more.

If only Troy were here to pick up the pieces.

Chapter Twenty-Eight

TROY

"Where were you all night?" I grumble at Marcus as he rolls into our room. "We have to leave for practice in like five minutes."

"What crawled up your ass this morning?" He brushes by, doing his best to ignore me.

"Maybe it's the fact that we have playoffs coming up and need to be in top shape."

Marcus shakes his head, grabbing his practice bag and throwing in a few things. "I'm here, aren't I? My game isn't suffering."

"If you have a couple more late nights it might. It's my job as captain to keep the team together."

Marcus pulls on his jacket and hefts his bag over his shoulder. "You really think the team mentality is, as you say, suffering?"

I huff. His nonchalant attitude is pissing me off. "You need to get serious about practice. Practice is where we earn our keep. We only have a few more weeks until playoffs start. Spending all night with some random chick isn't going to help us."

Fire lights his face. "Fuck you, Hollins. Harper isn't some random chick. I'm not getting my dick wet every other night with some bunny." He rubs his cheek with his middle finger. "Now let's get to practice. Wouldn't want the team to suffer because we show up late."

"Waiting on you, buddy."

This time, when he walks past me, he bangs into my shoulder.

Am I being an asshole to him?

Yes. There's no question. But while he's happy with Harper, I'm miserable. He doesn't know that Angie and I broke up. Because he's been too loved up with Harper.

And I kind of hate him for it.

Things have never been better for the two of them, and my life is crashing and burning.

Marcus is quiet the entire ride over to practice. When I pull into the parking lot, he's jumping out of my car when it's barely in park.

Not that I care. I don't feel anything.

It shows in my mood. I'm chippy. Missing easy passes and plays. Each time the puck misses my stick, I snap at the other guy. More than once a whistle is blown in my direction.

Each time it makes my blood boil more.

Until Marcus sends the puck my way and I miss it by a mile.

"What the fuck is wrong with you?" Marcus cross-checks me without much effort behind it.

"Me?" I shove him right back. "You missed an easy pass."

"You're the one that missed, not me. You've been off all week. What the hell is wrong with you?"

Marcus shoves me, this time with a little more force.

"Fuck off. I'm fine."

"You're obviously not, if you're going to be a little bitch about it."

I don't know why, but that sets me off. My fist collides with his chin with a loud crack.

"Oh shit! Fight!"

I don't know who calls it as Marcus returns my swing with one of his own.

"Why are you being such a dick?" he yells, his fist landing a solid hit on my cheek. No doubt it's drawn blood.

"Because you're being one!"

"What are you, five?"

Someone pulls me off him before I can get another swing in. There's an anger there that I've only seen directed at opposing teams.

"Hollins. Evans. My office. Now."

The deadly quiet to Coach's tone tells me that we're both fucked. Marcus is seething.

"Marcus—"

"Don't," he bites out. "Just...don't."

He skates off the ice, shoulders around his ears.

Shit. I've already lost Angie this week. There's no way I can lose him too.

Fuck.

Marcus heads to the locker room, but Coach Morris points directly at his office. I guess there's no changing before this beating.

I drop down into the chair beside Marcus in the tiny office. For a coach's office, it's sparsely decorated. Aside from a whiteboard covered in plays on one wall, there isn't much in here.

The slam of his door reverberates around us.

If I'm still on the team by the end of the day, I'd be shocked.

"Never, in all my years of coaching, have I seen my captain and alternate go after each other."

"It was my fault," I offer up immediately.

"Why?"

"I'm going—"

Coach holds up his hand, stopping me. "Save it. I don't actually want to hear it. There's no reason you could give me that would excuse your behavior today."

His eyes are murderous as he stares between the two of us.

"Are we going to be suspended?" Marcus asks.

"I should. I should kick both of you off the team. You know I don't put up with this. You're captains and seniors. You're supposed to set an example to the rest of the team. And you're fighting?"

"I'm sorry, Coach." It's all I can say.

"Tomorrow before practice. Every drill you hate—iron cross, lightning drills—you're doing all of them. Two hours early. Then practice. I don't plan on taking it easy on you."

"Yes, Coach," we answer in unison.

"Now get the hell out of my office. I don't want to see either one of you."

Fuck. Considering how much worse that could have been, I think suicide drills is basically getting off scot-free.

"Way to go, asshole," Marcus mutters as we enter the locker room. He ignores me as he grabs his stuff to hit the showers. With practice still going on, we're the only two in here.

All the fight has left my body as I slump into my stall and bang my head against the tiled wall.

Am I really going to let my entire future slip through my fingers because of Angie?

What kind of future do I have without her?

"Are you really just going to sit here and sulk? Jesus,

what the fuck is the matter with you?" Marcus chucks his towel into his own stall. Water drips from his hair, soaking his T-shirt. "Seriously. I'm done with this 'I'm fine' bullshit. If I'm dragging my ass out of bed for suicides tomorrow, I deserve to know why."

"Angie left."

That draws him back. There's a tiny cut on his jaw that's red. At least it's not bleeding. "What? No way."

I nod. I haven't said the words out loud. Because saying them out loud makes them true. I haven't wanted to face it yet.

"Her dads found out."

"Oh shit." His face pales. "How?"

"They showed up at her apartment and were there when we got back. It was bad."

"Why didn't you tell me?"

"Because I didn't want it to be real."

"So you decided to beat the shit out of me instead?"

I wince. "I deserve that."

"You're lucky I like you, you asswipe." Marcus gives me a friendly shove, the fight from earlier now forgotten.

At least that's the one good thing about our friendship. In all the years we've known each other, we don't let things fester.

If only I had talked to him instead of punching him to start with. Might have saved our asses tomorrow.

"What'd Angie have to say about all this?" Marcus sits on the bench next to me.

"She's been ignoring me."

"Ouch."

"Yeah." I drag a hand through my sweaty hair. "I don't know what else I can do. She's not answering my calls or texts. The last thing her dad asked was if she was going to pick me over her family."

"Troy. You should've told me this. That's fucked-up."

"Don't I know it." My laugh comes out bitter and depressed. "Angie's family is everything to her. I can't ask her to give them up for me."

"Why are they asking her to give you up at all?"

"They can't see past my father and their history."

Marcus shakes his head. "This isn't the Gladiator I know and love."

I bat my eyelashes at him. "Aww…you still love me?"

He pats my cheek in the way only a friend can. "Why, I don't know. But if you're going to act like a dick from here until eternity, you need to figure something out."

"How? It's either me or her family. There's no way she's picking me."

His answer to me is an eye roll. What an ass.

"Have you thought that maybe you should, I don't know, talk to her family?"

"Talk to them?"

"I know it's a novel idea, but yes, you idiot. If you love her as much as you say you do—"

I stab a finger at him, cutting him off. "I didn't say I loved her."

"So this is not for love then?" He points at his jaw.

My hands move on their own, thrown up in defeat. "Fine. Continue."

"If you love her like you say you do, you can't take this lying down. Reach out to her dad."

"But what if he won't listen?"

The smallest glimmer of hope blooms in my chest.

"Make him. You're not one to back down in the face of adversity. What, you give up in the third period when we're down by two?"

"No."

"That's right. Pull your head out of your ass, shower,

and then come up with a game plan." He stands, stretching his arms over his head as he always does after practice. "And then buy me dinner to make it up to me."

"I'm not buying your sorry ass dinner."

"You owe me." He points to his jaw. Again.

I laugh. Of course my best friend is going to be like this. He wouldn't be Marcus otherwise. "How long are you going to milk this?"

"Until you get Angie back."

"That's motivation if I ever needed some."

Except his words settle inside me as I hit the showers. Something about the steam helps clear my jumble of thoughts today.

I've been nothing but an ass to Marcus today. My dad still knows enough people that he could get me the information I need.

Just the thought of talking to Angie's dads scares the shit out of me. To say I didn't make a great first impression would be an understatement. But maybe if I tell them how much I love their daughter, they might hear me out.

It's my only shot. An overtime goal to win the Stanley Cup.

The only other option is to give up Angie once and for all.

And that's not a future I'm prepared for.

Chapter Twenty-Nine

TROY

"Are you sure about this?" Marcus asks. "What if it makes things worse than it is?"

"Worse? This was your idea, wasn't it?" I straighten my shirt.

I haven't talked to Angie in a week. Every call and text goes ignored. I have no idea what is going on with her and her dads.

Nothing good from what I can imagine. Walking out of her apartment that day was one of the hardest things I've ever had to do. But staying there with her mad family wasn't going to help matters.

"I don't know. They could tell you they hate you—and your dad—and never want you to see their daughter again."

"Like I haven't thought about that a hundred times. But what's the alternative? Fucking my way through practice because I don't have her anymore?"

A pain tugs in my chest.

I've never been more miserable in my entire life.

Hockey always used to be the distraction I needed when things in life got too hard.

Now it's not. And I don't know what to do. Especially if things don't go the way I want them to today.

"If you do that, then you don't have to worry about being drafted," Marcus jokes. It's the perfect tension breaker I need.

"Worried about the competition?"

"Yes. Because we're up for the exact same position in the draft." He rolls his eyes at me.

"Maybe that means we'll end up on the same team."

"That's almost too much to hope for."

I'd love nothing more than to get to play with Marcus in the NHL, but the odds of that are slim.

"We'll think about that later. I've got bigger things to worry about." Shrugging into my blazer, I turn to face Marcus. "How do I look?"

"Like you're going to ask me for money."

"Good then?"

"Yes. But I'm not giving you money."

"Then I guess you need to up your game to get draft-ed." I punch him in the arm before leaving our shared room.

Guys are lingering around the house with no practice this afternoon. Some are studying and others have already started pregaming for parties tonight.

"Cap! You want to join us?" One of the freshman holds out a beer to me.

"Can't. Might catch you later though."

If this meeting doesn't go as I'm hoping it will.

The drive is quiet as I head to the diner my dad and I always went to after my hockey games in high school. I figure if I'm going to do this, I might as well do it some-where I'm familiar with.

I give myself a pep talk the entire way over. It does little to quell the rising nerves. I've gone over everything I want to tell Angie's dads in my head. How much I love her and respect her and the relationship she has with them. How much my dad has changed and that he's not the same person he was during his playing days.

Will it work? I have no fucking clue. But I can't sit around any longer and let this thing fester. I can't keep fighting with Marcus. He's told me—through Harper, of course—that Angie isn't in a good place. And I know she won't feel better until she can make up with her dads.

The diner parking lot is half full as I pull in and park next to the familiar car. At least my parents are on time.

"Troy!" My mom's voice echoes in the quiet space from a booth in the back. So far, it's just the two of them.

Red plastic booths line the wall. The jukebox in the corner is playing an old tune. The smell of milkshakes and fries lingers in the air. Everything looks like it's straight out of the 1950s.

"Hey guys." I give my mom a hug before dropping into the seat next to them. Two half-empty coffee cups sit on the table.

"You look like you're going to be sick," Dad tells me.

"Derek. Not helpful." Mom elbows him in the side.

"Thanks for the vote of confidence."

"It's going to be okay," Mom says.

"What if it's not?" My voice is small. "What if it all goes to hell and I don't get Angie back?"

"What do I always say? Don't go borrowing trouble," Mom chides.

"I guess you're right." I blow out a nervous breath as the bell above the door jingles. Two imposing figures walk in.

"I guess it's now or never."

"It'll be okay," Dad tells me, reaching over to clasp my arm. His face looks as nervous as mine.

I stand from my seat, watching as their eyes scan the small diner. When Alex's gaze locks on mine, the feeling of wanting to puke comes back. His face is hard, not giving anything away.

He and Carter exchange a few words before they walk over.

Well, stalk over. Alex still doesn't look happy to be here. This isn't boding well for me.

"Troy."

"Mr. Brooks-Young," I say to both of them, not really knowing how to greet them otherwise. I shake their hands.

Maybe that's the sign of a promising start?

"I know you know my dad, but this is my mom, Sutton."

"It's nice to meet you both." She shakes their hands. "I've heard a lot about you both."

"I'm afraid we haven't had the pleasure yet." Carter's voice is warm as he drops down into the seat beside Alex.

The fact that he's sitting on the outside makes me think he might keep Alex in the booth if this goes sideways. At least I'm hoping that's what he's doing. He definitely seems to be the more reasonable of the two.

"You wanted to talk to us?" Alex sinks back into the plastic seat of the booth and crosses his arms.

"Alex, dear. Tone it down." Carter's voice is curt as he pats his arm. "Hear the poor kid out. He looks heartbroken."

He tries to whisper but does a bad job of it. At least I was right in that he seems to be on my side.

"I know I'm not your favorite person, but Angie is *my* favorite person. I love her more than you know, sir,"—that gets me a slight quirk of Alex's lips—"and I don't want our families' history to get between us."

"It's a fairly weighted history," Alex mumbles.

Carter reaches over and grabs his hand, pulling it into his lap.

"Mr. Brooks-Young—"

"Look, I'm the problem here," Dad interrupts. "Don't take it out on the kids."

"So I'm supposed to ignore you for the rest of my life?" Alex says. "You treated me like shit. Words have power, Hollins. You used yours to hurt people."

Carter shakes his head at him.

"I know." Dad hangs his head, staring at his coffee cup. "I was the worst kind of person to you, and I wanted to reach out and apologize to you more times than you can imagine."

I know all about my dad's past. He told me about it when I was in high school. If he hadn't told me, I wouldn't have believed him. He's not that same guy. I only hope that I can make Angie's parents see that. See the good person that he is. What a kind and loving man he is for his family.

Getting angry at him won't help the situation.

"Why didn't you?" Alex asks.

"Would it have made you feel better if I absolved myself? Besides, I didn't think you'd believe me."

Alex shrugs a shoulder. "I don't know if I would have. Especially back when we were still playing."

"Look, I know you have no reason to trust my words now, but I've changed." Dad reaches over and takes Mom's hand. "I've been working with your foundation at my high school."

"What?" This gets Alex's attention. "How did I not know about this?"

"Because I had my assistant coach do everything at the time. I didn't want people to know."

"Why not?"

"Because it wasn't about me. It was about helping others." Dad scrubs a hand over his brow. "I'm not proud of my playing days. Vegas was a hard team to play for and they rewarded dickish behavior. Encouraged it, even. I fed into it. The dirtier the better. When Troy came along, I realized that wasn't the kind of person I wanted to be. I didn't want to raise my son in that environment. The day he was born was the day I retired from the league. The things I said to you? I'm ashamed of myself and have done a lot of work to make sure I never make anyone else feel like that. Or any of my players."

"I can't get over that you're working with Team Rainbow." Alex messes with the rubber bracelet on his wrist that has his organization's name on it. "Not much gets by me there. It's my baby."

"I know how to be discreet when needed." Dad smiles at him. "I want us to be able to move past our history, Alex. I'm sorry for the things I said and did when I played. It might not mean much to you, but I truly am. And I hope you'll consider accepting it to let our children be happy. Troy here is a better man than I'll ever be."

"Remember what I told you," Carter reminds him. "Our daughter loves him."

Alex aims a soft look in his direction. "I know. Can't I let him stew for another minute? If he's not scared of me, then how will I threaten him that if he ever treats Angie badly I'll kill him?"

"You mean it?"

"You want to be threatened by him?" Carter asks me. "Really?"

"No, not that." I wave him off. "To get to treat her *any way* means I'd be with her to start with…"

I don't want to let myself hope. Even the tiniest sliver dangled in front of me and then pulled away would be too much for me to handle.

Folding his hands, Alex leans across the table.

"I guess I should be sorry too," Alex starts, looking at my dad. "I let our past color my opinion of you and your family. I know I'm not the same person I was twenty years ago, so I don't know why I wouldn't give you the benefit of the doubt. If my daughter approves, then I guess I can too."

"Are you serious? Like for real?"

"Yes," Carter confirms. "We didn't know you were the reason our daughter was so happy, but we've seen how happy she's been these last few months. That's all we want for her."

"I promise, I will treat her right. I love her more than anyone else on this planet, and I just want the chance to build a life with her."

This time, the smile Alex gives me is genuine and bright. "That's all we've ever wanted for her."

"All any parent wants," Mom agrees, eyes glassed over with tears. "You have a wonderful daughter, and I know how lucky Troy feels to be with her."

I nod at my mom's words. "Thank you for giving me the chance to show her I love her, Mr. Brooks-Young. And Mr. Brooks-Young."

Alex reaches across the table to shake my hand. "Call us Alex and Carter."

Carter's eyes are sparkling. "Now, tell us your plan to get our daughter back."

Chapter Thirty

ANGIE

"Why are you dragging me to the beach?"

Harper points her car in the direction of the coast, doing her best to ignore me. "Why not go to the beach?"

"Because it's fifty degrees outside. No one in their right mind goes to the beach this time of year."

She swats my leg. "I thought you were from Colorado and used to cold weather?"

"Sue me," I grumble. "I've gotten used to the warm weather here."

"I brought a coat for you. So quit your whining."

There's no point in arguing with her. Whether I want to go to the beach or not, she's taking me, kicking and screaming.

After the disaster of a party, I retreated to the safety of my apartment. It's the first time I've left the comfort of my room in a week besides class. Even going to class has been a struggle. Everywhere I go on campus reminds me of Troy. It makes me sad, then I get irrationally angry.

All because of my dads. For two people who run a

charity based on inclusivity and not judging people, they made up their minds about Troy without even getting to know him.

God, I'm so mad I could burst.

"Are you okay over there?" Harper asks, breaking me from my runaway train of anger.

"I'm fine," I snap back.

"Sure. The huffing and that tone tell me you are one hundred percent *fine.*"

"Look, what are we doing here? I'm really not in the mood."

Harper pulls the car into one of several open spots in the beach parking lot. The sun is dipping low against the water, orange and yellow giving way to dark blues. A family is flying a kite along the shore.

"Trust me, okay?" Harper reaches behind her and chucks my coat at me.

"Fine."

Pulling up my jeans, I trudge through the sand behind Harper. It's then I notice the group of people around a bonfire pit a ways down the beach.

"What in the world?"

"I had to get you here somehow." Harper winks at me before joining the crowd in front of me.

Troy. His family. My family and grandparents.

It's hard to focus on Troy when I see my dad and his dad talking.

"Hey." Troy's hands are stuffed in his hoodie pocket. The one that I loved wearing whenever I wasn't with him. Deep, purple bags sit under his eyes. He's doing about as well as I am from the looks of it.

God, I've missed him. How has it only been a week? It feels like it's been years since I've seen him.

"What's going on?" I ask him, hoping I can get a straight answer.

"A peace offering. If you'll take it."

"A peace offering?" I peer behind him, and everyone has stopped talking, now looking at the two of us.

I feel like I'm in a fishbowl with all these eyes on me.

"I love you, Angie, and I don't want you to have to choose between me and your family."

"But—"

"Can we talk, sweetheart?" Dad interrupts him.

I have half a mind to say no. I can be just as stubborn as he is. It's where I get it from.

"Okay."

Troy gives me a soft smile. One that causes butterflies to erupt in my stomach. I don't want it to. Because if this goes badly, I don't know if I'll ever recover from losing him.

I follow my dad down to the shore. The waves are rolling in, kissing the sand. I wrap my coat tighter around me as a cold breeze blows in off the water.

"Do you know what one of the hardest days of my life was?"

"What?" My brows pull together at the question. The hardest day of his life? "When Nick was born?"

"Funny," he says with a laugh. "The day I dropped you off for your first day of kindergarten."

"Really?"

My dad crosses his arms, staring out across the Pacific. His rainbow band is snug on his wrist. It matches the one that I'm wearing.

Even if I was pissed as hell at him—still am, for that matter—I didn't take it off.

His eyes are glassy when they turn to face me. "The best thing football gave me was the offseason and getting to be at home with you and your brother. I hated being away from you guys. Every season got harder and harder as you got older. But it wasn't until I dropped you off on your first day of school that it hit me."

"What?"

"You always told me I was your best friend. I knew it was something that you said because you loved me, but you said you were going to make five new friends and marched right into school without looking back."

"Sounds like me." I let out a watery laugh.

"I knew then that you were destined for great things. And it made me cry the entire way to practice that day. You have such a big heart, Angela, and I wanted to protect you for as long as I could because the world is a scary place. But it turns out, you don't need it. You found someone who will protect it with everything he has."

I stare down at my feet, sinking through the sand as the water continues rolling over them.

"When Troy reached out to us to try and make things right, I knew he was the man for you."

"Really?" I can't imagine how nervous Troy was for that conversation.

Dad nods. "I let my past get in the way of your future and for that, I'm sorry."

"My future?" That has my gaze snapping up to meet his. I'm the spitting image of him. I always have been. Right down to my personality.

"I misjudged Troy. He's not his father."

"You know his father isn't what you think he is, right?"

He blows out a breath. "I know. I was wrong about that too."

"What happened to not being part of the family?" My voice cracks. "Did you mean that?" I swipe at the stray tear that falls free.

"God no." Dad pulls me in for a hug. "I reacted badly, Angela. You are my daughter and I will always love you, even if you hate me for that for the rest of your life. I will forever be sorry for what I said and will understand if you can't forgive me."

"I didn't mean to hurt you," I whisper.

"You didn't, sweetheart. I didn't understand what a good man Troy was and how worthy he was to protect that big heart of yours."

"Yeah?" I look up at my dad. Tears are running down his face.

"Yeah. It might take some time, but I'm getting there. Derek isn't all that bad."

"You're going to try?"

"Yes. I promise I will keep my cool for as long as I can."

"And when will that run out?" I laugh against him.

"When he proposes. Can I lose my cool then?"

The thought of marrying Troy has my heart stumbling in my chest. Even though I know I want to, it's still a long way off. "Dad, we haven't even graduated. Let's not go there just yet."

"At least I have some time to prepare."

I squeeze him a little tighter. "I'm sorry too."

"Sweetheart, you have nothing to be sorry about. I overreacted."

"I wouldn't have done it if I didn't love him."

"I know, Angie. I know."

"Are we good over here?" Pops comes over.

"We're good." I pull him into our hug. "Dad said he was wrong."

"Has hell frozen over?" Pops asks.

"I can admit when I'm wrong."

"Doesn't happen often."

I laugh at the two of them. I don't know what I would've done if Troy hadn't done this. Would they have been big enough to do it themselves?

Family is the most important thing in my life, but so is Troy. And now I get both?

"Can I introduce you guys to Troy?"

Pops smiles down at me. "We've already met him."

Dad whacks him on the stomach. "Let her introduce us to her boyfriend."

"Do I have to meet him?" Nick whines from behind Pops. "I have an AP physics test Monday that I need to study for."

"You can study when we get back to the hotel, you little genius." Pops wraps his arm around Nick and pulls him into our little group.

The weight I've been carrying on my shoulders since Troy and I started this thing between us lifts. I never realized how much it was pushing me down. Like walking through quicksand. I love my family more than anything and wouldn't have jeopardized this—what we have right here—for anything less than true love.

And that's exactly what I found with the man walking to me now.

Chapter Thirty-One

TROY

"**A**m I interrupting?"

"Yes," Angie's younger brother, Nick, answers.

"Nick!" They all yell at him at the same time. I can't help but laugh because it's the exact same thing that Lydia and I would do.

"Troy, would you like to meet my dads? Officially, I mean," Angie clarifies.

Even though I've met them twice before now, they're still intimidating. An ex-NFL star who still looks like he could bench press me? Yeah, not intimidating at all.

"Yes." I wipe my hands on my jeans. Seriously, where are these nerves coming from?

"Troy, this is my dad, Alex, and my pops, Carter."

I shake both of their hands. "It's nice to officially meet my girlfriend's dads."

"It's nice to meet you too."

"What are your intentions with our daughter?" Carter asks.

"Uhh…"

Is he being serious? I thought that was pretty obvious by now.

"Carter, leave him alone. Hasn't he already been through enough?" Alex laughs.

"Don't scare him off now." Angie's eyes are sparkling.

"Mr. Brooks-Young—"

"What did I tell you? Call us Alex and Carter."

"Would you mind if I talked to Angie?"

I glance over at her, drinking my fill of her. The time we spent apart was too much. It made me realize that my life would never be complete without her. She looks as wrecked as I am.

Alex nods at me. "We'll give you two a minute."

"Can I go study now?"

"Yes, you can go study. But grab a hot dog while you're at it," Carter yells after her brother.

Angie is glowing in the setting sun. I don't think I've ever seen her this happy. Now that our secret is out to her family, she doesn't have to hide anymore. It can be the two of us together.

Linking my hand with hers, I walk us down to the shore where the tide is rolling in. Her hand is warm in mine against the cool breeze. Long brown hair is whipping around her face.

"How did you get them all here together?" Angie wraps her arms around my waist, pulling me close. Her eyes are red-rimmed.

"Once I got them all together the first time, it was easy."

"And how'd you pull that off?"

"Easy. I called them."

Except it was the hardest call I ever made in my life. Because if they had said no, I don't know what I would have done.

"You called Pops, didn't you?"

I laugh, squeezing her even closer to me. "Fuck yeah. Your dad still scares the crap out of me."

"Once you get to know him, he'll be okay."

"I'm glad I have the chance."

Angie looks up at me. She's not wearing an ounce of makeup. This Angie might be my favorite. The one very few people get to see.

Only me.

"I'm sorry how they found out about us." I brush my fingers over her cheek. I'm memorizing her face all over again.

"I'm glad they came to their senses," Angie tells me. "I love you, Troy. We wouldn't be here today if it weren't for you."

"I don't know. I think you might have convinced them."

She shakes her head. "They got to see why I love you so much. You fought for the two of us when I don't know if I could have."

I cup her cheeks in my hands, dropping my forehead to hers. Her skin is so soft. Agonizingly soft. I want to take her back to her place and be with her. Say fuck it to our families that are here on the beach with us.

But I can't. At least not right now.

"I will always fight for you, Angie. Whatever happens, it's going to be you and me."

Angie presses up on her toes and gives me the sweetest kiss of my life. It sends heat rolling through me.

I keep it light and easy. I don't want her dads hating me already.

Angie breaks the kiss, licking her lips. "I like the sound of that."

"You know I won't know where I'm going until the draft."

"Doesn't matter."

"I could go to Nashville."

Angie shudders. "Then we'll go to Nashville. And you'll be the best damn player the Knights have ever had."

"You'd be okay with that?"

"Like you said. As long as we're together, I don't care where we end up."

"God, I love you."

The smile she gives me lights up her entire face. "I'll never get tired of hearing you say that to me."

"I'll tell you every single day. You might get sick of it."

The tide rushes in around us, soaking our pants. "Never. I will never get tired of hearing how much you love me, Troy."

Grabbing her around the waist, I swing her around and run farther out into the water. "Even if I drop you in the water?"

"Don't you dare!" she shrieks, trying to climb up my body.

"So there's a limit on how much you love me?"

"I'll love you even if you drop me in the ocean."

I hike Angie up my body, wrapping her legs around me. "Then it's a good thing I don't want you to freeze all night."

"That makes you the best boyfriend there is."

"You know that title is eventually going to need an upgrade."

"Oh yeah?"

I nod, dragging my nose along her jaw before nipping at her ear. "I plan on making you mine forever."

"Forever, huh? That sounds like a pretty good deal to me."

Fiancée. Wife. Mother. I want everything life has to offer with Angie. Even though it's going to be a crazy few years with hockey consuming every minute, I want to give her everything.

Because she deserves it.

She's the kindest, most loving person I know, and there is nothing I wouldn't do for her.

"Are you two going to stay down there all night?" Dad calls behind me. "Food is getting cold."

"I guess we should probably join the party," Angie whispers, sliding down my body.

I don't let her leave though. "As soon as we get back, I'm having my way with you."

"Good. Because I'm ready." She winks at me before running back up to where our families are waiting.

Teasing little minx. I watch her as I follow in her path, happiness radiating off her. Angie said she'd follow me anywhere, but I can't help but think that I'm going to be the one trailing after her.

Angela Brooks-Young is the most captivating person I've ever met. She draws people in with her kindness and big heart. She's sexy without even trying.

I don't know how I got so lucky to have her fall for me, but I won't waste a second of our time together. It's going to be the two of us taking on the world.

"Hot dog?" Carter asks, breaking me from my thoughts.

"If you break Angie's heart, he'll probably poison it," Nick tells me, matter-of-factly.

"Ignore him."

"Thanks." I take the hot dog he's offering with a nervous laugh. "No poisoning will be necessary."

"Poisoning won't be needed." Alex comes up next to me and slings his arm around my shoulder.

"It won't. Because I don't plan on breaking Angie's heart."

"You won't," Alex confirms. "And if you do, I'll just strangle you with my bare hands."

He walks away, my jaw hitting the sand.

"Alex! Can you not scare him away?" Carter shakes his head. "I promise, we like you. You make our daughter happy."

"That's all I want to do."

"Good." Carter claps me on the shoulder and heads over to where Alex is talking with my dad.

"Is it just me, or is it weird to see them all laughing together?" Angie appears beside me.

"Not just you."

I never thought I'd see this. Alex is stubborn. No doubt where Angie gets it from. But I had to try something. My dad isn't who he used to be, and I'm glad they both came around to that way of thinking.

"We'll have to get used to it."

Her face is happy and glowing and I don't think I'll ever get tired of seeing it that way.

"Can I give a toast?" Alex interrupts us.

"Is a toast really necessary?" Nick chirps from his spot on the bench. "I'm trying to study."

"You can give a toast, Dad," Angie tells him, ignoring her brother.

"Toasts are kind of his thing," Carter says from his side.

Alex huffs out an awkward laugh. "I never thought I'd see the day where our two families would be here, gathering together."

"Never in a million years." Dad's laugh is just as awkward.

"But now that we're here together, I find that I actually like you, Derek."

"Thanks?" It comes out as more of a question than anything.

"Is there an actual toast in here?" Nick asks.

"Are you sure you want to join this family?" Angie whispers from her spot next to me. The sun is dipping lower, and the bonfire casts long fingers of light across the sand. Carter pulls Nick to the side, no doubt telling him to let his dad get through this.

"Sorry, bud," Alex tells him. "Troy, I know you'll be a wonderful partner for our daughter. Not many people would want to take us on, but you did. I wasn't the most welcoming person to you, and for that, I am sorry. Seeing you and Angie together, I know you two are meant for each other. I don't know what the future holds for you, but you'll face it together. And have both your families at your side supporting you. We love you both."

Angie leaves my side to go hug her dad then my parents. This is more than I ever could have hoped for. I have no doubt that they're going to be best friends before long.

"You know he's going to be your biggest fan, right?" Carter comes over to me now. He was the easier sell of the two of them. "Prepare to be smothered."

"If it means you're on my side, smother away."

"You might live to regret those words."

"Nah. We'll all be family soon enough."

"That's good to hear." This is Alex now, coming over to stand next to his husband. "Because we're not going to scare you away."

"I don't scare easy."

"Then welcome to the family, Troy." Alex shakes my hand.

"Thanks. I'm glad to be a part of it."

And it's true. There might be some growing pains as we navigate our new normal, but this is our future. With our families at our side.

It's all we could have ever asked for because we never knew if it would happen.

Romeo and Juliet have nothing on us.

True love with Angie?

It'll be the easiest thing in the world.

Chapter Thirty-Two

TROY

"Fucking champs, baby!" Randy jumps over me as he reaches for another shot.

"Shouldn't you be taking it easy?" I sip on my beer, watching the team celebrate around me.

"C'mon, cap. Don't be a party pooper."

The bar is packed with wall-to-wall people. No doubt everyone told everyone they know in town that we were celebrating at the bar in the lobby of our hotel. It's not the place where a rowdy group of hockey players should be. Glass shelves line the wall, backlit with bottles of expensive liquor. Colorful tiles cover the walls that match the glass-blown lamps hanging down from the ceiling. Yellow stools line the bar.

"Not being a party pooper. Just taking it easy."

"Fucker." He shoves off me before joining a group of juniors at the bar. I'm sure he is trying to convince them to go out to a club.

It's just after ten. It's not even that late, but the adrenaline from the game is starting to wane. The last thing I want to do is head out into the frigid Minneapolis night.

An early spring cold front swept through, and it snowed overnight, causing Angie and her family to get in late.

Thank God they made it for the game. I don't know if I would have been able to play as well as I did if she wasn't there.

"We're heading out." Dad claps me on the shoulder.

"Already? You really are getting old."

"Love you too, son." He pulls me in for a hug. "Don't overdo it tonight."

"I won't."

"We're so proud of you, Troy." Mom drops a kiss on my cheek, then pulls back. I don't let her get far, wanting a hug from her.

"It's all because of you two."

Emotion clogs my throat, not for the first time tonight. I don't know where I would be without her and my dad. Sutton supported me every step of the way. If Dad wasn't there, she was. Early morning practice, late night games, and everything in between.

This win is as much theirs as it is mine.

"You sweet, sweet boy. I love you." Tears well in her eyes.

"I love you, Mom and Dad."

"We love you," Dad says, his voice tight.

"Don't have too much fun." Mom points a finger at me as Dad pulls her out of the bar.

"Harper and I are going to head out too." Marcus appears at my side.

"Are you sure you don't want to have another drink?" I sling an arm around Marcus, pulling him back toward the table where Harper and Angie are waiting for us. "When are we going to get to celebrate a national championship ever again?"

"You're starting to sound like Randy."

"Sue me for wanting to celebrate with my best friend and co-captain."

"Technically alternate."

"Whatever. One more. That's it."

"Don't you want to celebrate with the girls?" Marcus's eyes drift back behind me to the table where I know they are.

"Of course. One more though. Don't leave me hanging."

"Fine. But just one."

There's a warmth buzzing through my veins. I haven't overdone it on the drinks tonight. Angie got her own room tonight, as did Harper, so we can all have some privacy.

There will be plenty of time for celebrating with Angie. This is a moment I will be reliving for the rest of my life.

Beating Boston in the Frozen Four championship— seeing Angie's ex pout his way off the ice—was more than I could have asked for.

Kissing her on center ice after we got the trophy? I don't know if anything will ever compare.

Maybe a Stanley Cup, but that remains to be seen. Knowing she was in the stands, knowing my entire family and her dads and brother were in the stands, made me up my game. I didn't want to leave college with any regrets. Not winning the championship would have stung.

So to win in epic fashion—coming back from two down in the third period—made it that much sweeter.

"Two shots of tequila." I wave the bartender over and order us each one last shot.

"Tequila? Really, dude?" Marcus eyes me warily.

"What? Worried you won't be able to get it up?"

"Fuck you." There's not bite to his tone as he smiles back at me. "I just want to be with Harper right now."

"I'm right here." A voice startles him from behind. "You can spend the night with Troy. It's fine."

"But what if I want to spend it with you?"

Dude is a total goner for Harper. Not that I can blame him. I'm the exact same way with Angie, who has just wrapped her arms around me.

"Want to get me a shot?" Her eyes are glassy. Not from too much alcohol from celebrating, but from exhaustion. With the weather in Minneapolis, their flight got delayed and they didn't land until early this morning. We'll be here for another day or so, but I know she's ready to pass out.

The bartender drops ours off, and I order one more for her. He's already there with the bottle, pouring two more with limes on the side. "For both the ladies. This round's on the house."

"Thanks, man."

I hand the shots out and look at the little group of people gathered around me. I never expected to be here at the beginning of the year. In a hotel bar in Minneapolis celebrating our big victory.

"I can't imagine getting to celebrate this with anyone else. We fought hard to be in this game. I love getting to play the sport I love with some of my best friends."

"Some of?" Marcus quirks his brow at me.

"Fine. My best friend. And to have you two here"—I look at Angie and Harper—"makes it all the sweeter. This has been quite the year for all of us."

Angie squeezes closer, brown eyes gazing up at me with so much love it steals the rest of my words. I only hold out the tiny glass and clink it with everyone else's.

"Cheers." Marcus and Harper echo, drinking their shots before setting down the empty glasses and sucking on the limes. Marcus pats me on the back and says, "Now, if you'll excuse us, the lady and I are getting out of here."

"Night!" Harper's giggles can be heard as the two of them rush out of the bar.

"So much for celebrating with him," I mutter, shaking my head at how loved up my best friend is.

"Will I do?" Angie sinks more into my side.

"Do?" I lift her into my arms and set her on the barstool. "Let me get the check and I'm taking you straight to bed."

I flag down our bartender and get the bill.

"I'm down for some fun, I promise," Angie says around a yawn.

"Okay, Miss Brooks-Young. You're the picture of wanting to party right now."

"You want to go out? I can go out." Angie tries to stand, but one push of my finger and she's collapsing back onto the stool.

Grabbing some bills out of my wallet, I hand them to the bartender and grab Angie's hand.

"The only place we're going is to our room."

"Party for two?" She waggles her brows at me as she skips ahead.

"With you? Every night is a party."

"Aww, you know how to say the sweetest things."

The hotel lobby is quiet as the elevator doors slide open and we step in. It's blissfully empty.

Wrapping my arms around her, I pull her toward me and lean against the elevator wall. Angie's brown eyes are tired. I know she stayed out late tonight just for me, and it makes me love her all the more for it.

"I'm so glad you were here today."

"There is nowhere else I'd rather be, Troy. Watching you play is one of my favorite things in the world."

"Really?"

Angie circles a finger around the buttons on my shirt. I

didn't change after we left the game. We came straight to the bar for our celebration. "You should know how much I love watching you play by now."

"I never thought I'd convert you to a hockey fan," I laugh.

"I'm a fan of yours. If you played competitive dodge-ball, I'd be a fan of the sport."

"You know you're going to have to be at every game from now on, right?"

"Every game?" She quirks a brow up at me before burrowing into my arms.

"Can't blame a guy for wanting to have the woman he loves around. You're my good luck charm."

"I thought you didn't believe in that?"

The elevator dings and opens up on our floor. I have my arm around Angie's waist to keep her upright. Both of us are ready to pass out.

Pulling the keycard out of my wallet, I hold it over the door until it beeps and lets us in. We go about getting ready for bed, exhaustion blanketing us. Between the travel and the game, we're running on fumes.

Grabbing the neck of my T-shirt, I pull it over my head and drop it on the couch before flopping down on the bed. Angie, in one of my SDU T-shirts, curls up next to me, one leg thrown over my hips.

"I love you, Angie."

She presses a kiss into my bare chest. "Not as much as I love you."

"Doubtful."

Angie brushes a finger over my jaw. "Do you think it's always going to be like this? Just the two of us?"

Her eyes are drifting closed.

"It might be hard, but I promise you, I will do every-thing to give you the life you deserve."

"All I want is you, Troy."

Her heavy breath ghosts over my chest and I know she's asleep. Having her here in my arms puts a sleepy smile on my face.

I don't know how I got so lucky. I never thought I would find this. I figured I would go through college, going through the motions. Maybe find someone who I wanted to date.

But Angie?

I never expected her. She's everything I ever wanted in life. Getting drafted is both exciting and scary. I don't know what the future holds, but I know with her by my side, it's going to be easier. The scary times less hard. The good times even better. That's what our love is.

It's that thought that carries me off to sleep.

A future with Angie.

I can't fucking wait.

Epilogue

"Y ou look great, son." Dad brushes an imaginary piece of lint off of my shoulder. "Any team would be lucky to have you."

"I know." The smile I give him is nervous.

I can't help it.

The big night is finally here.

Night one of the NHL draft.

I've talked with a few teams, but I still have no idea where I'm going to end up. The dream?

Denver. The Colorado Black Diamonds are the top team. The one every player dreams will draft them.

"Is it wrong to say I won't cheer for you if you play for Nashville?" Lydia asks, scrolling through her phone.

Since she arrived, my sister has done nothing but look at the stats and which team is likely going to pick which player. Thankfully, she finally stopped saying it to me. Which is good, because I can only handle hearing about other players so much.

"Lydia, you will cheer for your brother wherever he

285

ends up," Mom interjects and then shushes her. "Just like he cheers for you."

"Shows what you know," she whispers.

"*If* you go to Nashville, then we'll all get jerseys and wear them at your first home game. Right, Angie?" Dad turns to Angie, who's been standing in the corner of our hotel room.

"You couldn't keep me away." Her smile is beaming.

"Can you guys give us a minute?" I ask my family.

I love them, but with them around, it's only making me more nervous.

"Sure thing. We'll wait for you downstairs," Dad tells me.

"Don't take too long. We don't want to be late."

"Sutton. We won't be late."

They argue about when the car will be here as they walk out the door of our suite.

"How are you feeling?"

Sunbeams shine through the windows of our hotel room. The Strip is bustling below us. Vegas is alive with energy. Fans from all over the country have come to see which players are going to which team.

But I couldn't care less because of the woman standing in front of me. She looks sexy as hell with her brown hair pulled back into a complicated twist off her neck and a simple black dress.

"Shouldn't I be asking you that?" Angie clasps her soft hands around my neck.

"It's your future too."

"I like the sound of that."

I drop my forehead to hers. "The future?"

She nods, pressing a warm kiss to my lips. "*Our* future."

And to think, we might not even be here if I hadn't

convinced her dads to give my family a chance. Everything I've ever wanted is within my grasp.

A hockey career. Playing for a team I love.

Angie.

I never realized how much I needed someone like her until she came into my life. She's everything I never knew I needed.

No matter which team I end up with, I know I'll be okay. Because I'll have Angie by my side.

"I have a little something for you," I tell her.

"Oh yeah?" Warm, brown eyes gaze up at me, and fuck if it doesn't make me weak in the knees.

"Hang on."

I leave her and rush into my room to grab the small black box. Angie's moved onto the sofa, kicking off her red heels.

"You know we have to leave in a few minutes, right?" I drop down onto the cushion next to her.

"And if I have to wear heels all night, then I'm going to sit for a few minutes." She drops her legs over my lap. "Now, what's this little something you have for me?"

Grabbing her hand, I set the velvet box in it. "It's nothing big."

She snaps open the box and her jaw drops.

"Nothing big? Troy, it's beautiful."

She pulls out the small, gold locket. The heart engraved on it is worn down, no doubt from years of wear. "It was my grandma's."

Angie clicks open the locket, eyes watering at the pictures inside.

"No matter where you go, our families will always be with us."

"Troy. I love it."

She fingers the two pictures inside. One of both our

families from that day at the beach and the other of the two of us from my last hockey game at SDU. I'm a sweaty mess, but she's in my arms. Kissing me like it's the last thing she'll do.

Which is something I don't have to think about. Because whatever happens tonight, we'll be together.

"I love you, Angie. And wherever we end up tonight, it's you and me."

"Always." She cups my cheeks in her hands, the cool metal of the locket pressing against my freshly shaven jaw, and kisses me.

I hold her close as her tongue slides into my mouth. Savoring the taste of her, I let myself get swept up in the moment. Because from here on out, it's going to be nothing but craziness.

Angie pulls back, nipping at my bottom lip. "I love you."

My phone buzzes in my pocket. No doubt it's one of my parents telling us to get a move on.

"We need to go." I sigh.

"Wait. Put it on me." She passes it back to me to secure around her neck. It sits just below the star necklace I got her for Christmas.

Angie slips back into her shoes and links her hand with mine. "Whatever happens tonight, Troy, we're together."

I sweep a stray hair behind her ear. "I love you."

And we head out of the room, leaving our old life behind us.

ANGIE

Chaos. It's the only way to describe the atmosphere at the convention center tonight.

Players from all over the country—the world, really—are here tonight. Hoping for a shot at being drafted by one of the elite teams.

Troy and I have been in town all week with his family. My nerves have been growing with each passing day. Lydia has been giving me every prospective player's stats.

Considering that my pops is a math teacher and I grew up knowing football stats, I understand them all.

And my only goal tonight is to try and be as calm as possible. Because I don't want Troy to be nervous.

"Troy, can we get a quick word before the draft starts?" a reporter asks.

I squeeze his hand. "I'll meet you backstage."

"Love you," he mouths. I do the same and head off to find our families.

"Angie. You doing okay?"

Dad's waiting with Derek, the two of them now friends. I never thought they'd become friends as fast as they did, but they have.

"If I tell you I'm fine, would you believe me?"

"Not at all," Pops laughs.

"Then maybe if I say it enough, I'll start to feel it."

"You won't," Derek tells me. "I puked before I was drafted."

"Derek, that's not helping." Sutton slaps him on the stomach.

"Actually, it kind of does."

No matter how much I've discussed this with my dad and Troy, I know anything can happen tonight. Teams can trade up for a better position. All the conversations in the world are meaningless until he gets the call.

Until his name is announced on the stage.

"Is it weird for you to be announcing the hockey draft pick?" Derek asks my dad.

"Must be a slow week if they're bringing in ex-football players to liven up hockey."

"I still don't know where I went wrong with him. Hockey over football?"

Warm arms wrap around my shoulders, pulling me against a broad chest I'm so familiar with. "You're still going on about me picking hockey over football?"

"Yes," both my dad and Derek answer.

"Football is unequivocally the best sport on the planet," Dad says.

"If you had to pick a sport outside of football, I guess hockey is okay." Derek rolls his eyes in a playful way.

Not the first time I've heard this conversation. And it won't be the last.

"Troy, first pick is up soon. Time to settle in."

"Now I'm nervous." Troy pulls me even closer, pressing a kiss to the crown of my head.

"It's okay." I squeeze his forearms. "We've got this."

Troy spins me in his arms. "We do. We've got this."

"Are you trying to reassure yourself, or me?"

"Me." He laughs.

All of us find a seat at our table. This part will be the worst. The sitting and waiting. Troy's talked with several teams, the Colorado Black Diamonds included. Tonight could go one of several ways.

What Troy doesn't know is that I've been looking at places for the both of us in each city. I hate not knowing where we'll be, but as long as we're together, I'll be happy.

With the draft starting, things don't calm down. If anything, the tension is palpable. A living, breathing thing. Every single person in here is wanting to hear their name called. Some will go home ecstatic. Others will be disappointed.

Phones ring and cameras pan around the room. They hope to catch that flash of emotion of not getting picked by the team they were hoping to be called to.

I only hope we're not in the latter because I know how hard Troy has worked. He deserves his shot in the big leagues as much as any other person here.

A young staffer comes over to our table. "Mr. Young. We need you now."

"I'll see you guys when I'm done." Dad claps me on the shoulder as he stands to leave. "Troy, don't get drafted while I'm gone."

"No promises," he says with a grin.

"How are you holding up?" Troy leans closer to me, his dark eyes studying my face. He looks as handsome as ever in his gray suit.

"I wish they would hurry up and call your name. I'm dying."

He gives me a crooked smile. It has butterflies gathering in my stomach. Almost a year later and he still has the same effect on me.

The TV screens light up as my dad is called on stage.

"To announce the Black Diamonds' first pick of the draft, we welcome Hall of Fame quarterback from the Denver Mountain Lions, Alex Young."

"Holy shit," Troy murmurs.

He holds up his phone screen. A Denver area code.

"No way." I clasp my hands over my mouth as my dad walks out on stage. This can't be happening right now, can it?

Are the Black Diamonds going to draft Troy?

"This is Troy," he answers the call as my dad starts speaking.

"Tonight, I'm here to announce Colorado's first pick of the draft. I know what you're thinking. Why is a football player announcing the first pick in the hockey draft?"

The audience breaks out in laughter.

"Okay, that sounds great." Troy's face is lit up.

"It's nice to know I still have some pull when I heard who my hometown team would be drafting. And tonight, I have the great honor of announcing the newest member of the Black Diamonds. Now, I might be biased, but I think this young man is going to go far and bring a few championships home to the city we love."

"Troy…" I whisper with a gasp.

He's beaming and not saying a word as a camera flashes to him.

"The Colorado Black Diamonds select center, number twenty-two from San Diego University, Troy Hollins."

"Why didn't he tell us?" Lydia asks from across the table. Sutton and Derek are jumping up and cheering, louder than anyone in the room.

"Because you can't keep a secret," Derek chides her.

"Did you know?" she asks her dad.

"I didn't. I wouldn't have been able to keep it secret either."

I don't hear their words as I leap into Troy's arms. "We're going to Denver!" I want to stay here all night, but I know I can't. Tears are streaming down my face.

Thank God for waterproof mascara.

"You didn't know, did you?" I ask, peppering his face with kisses.

"I had an inkling," Troy admits.

"Why didn't you tell me?"

"Because you can't keep a secret either!" Lydia calls from across the table.

"Troy, you're needed on stage." A staffer comes over to us, pointing out where he needs to go.

"We'll celebrate when you get back," I tell him, giving him one last kiss. Sutton and Derek give him a quick hug before he's walking across the stage and meeting my dad. The two of them share a hug that sends me soaring.

I never thought this would happen. That I'd get to keep Troy and my family. That we'd be going back to Denver. Together.

It's everything I want.

Best kept secret indeed.

THE END

Keep reading for a special bonus scene with Angie and Troy!

Bonus Scene

"God, I'm nervous."

"I wasn't, and look how that turned out."

I wince, grabbing Harper's hand. "You sure you're doing okay?"

She waves me off. "Yes. I'm fine. Just because I didn't get my happy ending, doesn't mean I'm not happy for you."

"I can't believe the day is here."

Two long years.

Troy proposed to me after his rookie season. While he didn't get much playing time, the time he was on the ice, he dominated. Between my work and his schedule, the off season is the only time that worked. If it were up to me, we would've gone down to city hall to get married.

But when we voiced that thought to our parents, it was swiftly ignored.

Both dads wanted to walk me down the aisle. Derek wanted to give a speech.

We opted for a small backyard wedding at my parents house.

With the attention Troy has been getting after this season, we didn't want a big affair splashed all over the gossip rags.

Our families and closest friends. That's it.

And not even all of them can make it.

"I'm just glad Marcus won't be here," I hear Harper whisper.

"Is everyone ready?" Sutton interrupts us before I can get more out of Harper.

"How's Troy doing?" I ask.

She's positively beaming. "Ready to see you. Angie, honey, you look beautiful."

Not for the first time today, my eyes start to water.

The dress is everything I imagined it would be. Hand-sewn lace stretches across my chest, with a low dip. The material hugs my hips before flowing out around my ankles.

"I can't believe it's finally here."

Sutton smiles, wiping her eyes. "He said the same thing."

Butterflies are dancing in my stomach. Even though it's small, I'm still nervous.

"Are my dads ready?"

"Yes. They want a minute with you before you head out."

"Okay." I turn to Harper. "How do I look?"

The smile she gives me is equal parts happy and sad. "Like you're ready to get married."

"I am."

They both give me a quick hug before my dads come in. Even though we're getting married in their backyard, they're both in all black suits with pale blue ties. A small nod to the Black Diamonds colors.

It matches the blue hydrangeas in my bouquet.

"Angela." Dad's voice catches as he scrubs a hand over his jaw. "I don't think I've ever seen you happier."

More tears.

"We couldn't have asked for a better man for you," pops tells me.

They pull me in for hug, squeezing extra hard.

"It's hard to believe you're all grown up and getting married." Dad wraps an arm around my shoulders, keeping me close. "I remember when you used to have pretend weddings in the living room."

I laugh. "I think I was marrying my stuffed mountain lion."

"Which I'm sure is still sitting in the attic," pops says.

"Are you ready?" I ask them.

They share a look. One full of love. The kind of love I hope Troy and I will have at their age.

"As ready as we'll ever be."

Grabbing my bouquet, we leave the office and walk through the house to the backyard.

The wall of family photos has grown over the years. Nick playing hockey. Our families at Troy's national championship. The night he proposed.

I never thought we'd get here. That our two families would be closer than ever and our dads as thick as thieves.

When we step out onto the porch, the backyard takes my breath away. Flowers cover every surface, wrapped around the beams of the pergola. Lights sparkle from the fence. Our closest friends are seated in a few chairs – my godparents and my dad's old teammates, Derek and Sutton, Lydia and her fiancée, and then there's Troy.

It has my steps faltering. I can't keep the tears at bay. I've never seen him look more handsome in my life. In a light gray suit with a light blue tie and his hair styled to perfection, I drink my fill.

I can see his tears through my own as we get closer.

"Slow down, Ang," Pops whispers into my ear.

"Sorry." I face him, squeezing his hand.

"I seem to recall you were the same way," Dad says over my head.

"Who could blame me?"

"Are you two ready to give me away?" I laugh as we get to the end of the aisle. Troy is waiting not so patiently.

"We'll never give you away, sweetheart," Dad tells me. "Our family is just getting bigger."

Dad and Pops each give me a kiss and hug before shaking hands with Troy.

"You look beautiful." Troy gives me a kiss on the cheek before we stand in front of the priest.

The ceremony goes by in the blink of any eye. Troy and I wanted a traditional ceremony, nothing fancy. I knew I would be too emotional to try and remember any words to say to Troy.

It doesn't matter. The two of us tell each other everyday how much we mean to one another. How much we love each other.

"Now, with the power vested in me by the state of Colorado, I know pronounce you husband and wife. You may kiss your bride."

Troy is beaming at me as he pulls me in for the best kiss of my life. One that seals our love forever. Through thick and thin. Whatever this life will throw at us.

We'll have our families by our sides, but Troy is it for me. I never expected to fall in love with this man, but he pulled me in.

And never let me go.

His eyes are wet as he drops his forehead to mine.

"I love you, Angela Brooks-Young Hollins."

I laugh, throwing my head back and linking hands with him. "That's a mouthful. Let's go with Angela Hollins."

"Angela Hollins. I love you, Angela Hollins."

Hugs are given as we walk down the small aisle to the back porch.

I pull him in for one last kiss before the caterers will start to set the party up. Butterflies swoop in my stomach at how perfect this kiss is.

It leaves me breathless.

"Better than all the stars in the universe?" I whisper against his lips. Whoops and cheers can be heard all around us.

Troy smiles, cupping my cheek.

"Better than every star in every universe in every galaxy."

Want to read about Angie's dads? Read Sideline Infraction now!

Author's Note

Book seventeen is out in the world!!

Y'all…I have been bursting at the seams to bring you this new world! This idea came to be one night as I was writing Sideline Infraction. What better idea for a story than feuding sports families?! I was so nervous starting this book and diving into hockey. I love reading second gen series and started laying the groundwork for these characters when writing the Mountain Lions. I hope you love these characters as much as I do! Get ready for a new season of the Black Diamonds!

There are a lot of people I need to thank for this book. To my beta readers Trish and Menotah, thank you for your help in making this book perfect! To Tina…you're more than just my PA and I love you more than London! My dad and his hockey friends were the ones who helped me come up with the team name — Black Diamonds. Outside of that? I'm not sure I wanted to take much of their advice (like their title ideas which will make an appearance in a future book it's that terrible :P) but the team name was gold! I want to thank my tribe. The people that I text when I have any sort of news, good, bad or amazing…Swati, Lily, Claire, Suzanne, Maria…I love you ladies more than you'll ever know!

To my Street Team and the Silver Society…I love getting to share my books with you and your excitement for them. And to all the readers, bookstagramers and booktokers….thank you for sharing and loving on my books and characters! You have made this the most incredible journey of my life and we're only just getting started!

<3 Emily

Also by Emily Silver

Colorado Black Diamonds Hockey

Best Kept Secret

Best Laid Plans - coming April 18, 2024

Best of the Best - coming summer, 2024

Best of Both Worlds - coming fall, 2024

Dixon Creek Ranch

Yours to Take

Yours to Hold

Yours to Be

Yours to Forget

Yours To Lose

The Denver Mountain Lions

Roughing The Kicker

Pass Interference

Sideline Infraction

Illegal Contact

The Big Game

Off the Deep End — A standalone, MM sports romance

The Ainsworth Royals

Royal Reckoning

Reckless Royal

Royal Relations

Royal Roots

Royal Ties

The Love Abroad Series

An Icy Infatuation

A French Fling

A Sydney Surprise

Love Under An Italian Sky - a newsletter freebie

Get the trope guide on my website, or
scan the QR code to read all my books on Kindle Unlimited

About the Author

After winning a Young Author's Award in second grade, Emily Silver was destined to be a writer. She loves writing inclusive stories, with strong heroines and the swoony men who fall for them.

A lover of all things romance, Emily started writing books set in her favorite places around the world. As an avid traveler, she's been to all seven continents and sailed around the globe.

When she's not writing, Emily can be found sipping cocktails on her porch, reading all the romance she can get her hands on and planning her next big adventure!

Find her on social media to stay up to date on all her adventures and upcoming releases!